Lily's Passport to Paris

Other Books Available

The Lily Series
Here's Lily!
Lily Robbins, M.D. (Medical Dabbler)
Lily and the Creep
Lily's Ultimate Party
Ask Lily
Lily the Rebel
Lights, Action, Lily!
Lily Rules!
Rough & Rugged Lily
Lily Speaks!
Horse Crazy Lily
Lily's Church Camp Adventure
Lily's in London?!
Lily's Passport to Paris

Nonfiction
The Beauty Book
The Body Book
The Buddy Book
The Best Bash Book
The Blurry Rules Book
The It's MY Life Book
The Creativity Book
The Uniquely Me Book
The Year 'Round Holiday Book
The Values & Virtues Book
The Fun-Finder Book
The Walk-the-Walk Book
NIV Young Women of Faith Bible

Lily's Passport to Paris

❋

Z ZONDERVAN®

ZONDERVAN.com/
AUTHORTRACKER
follow your favorite authors

ZONDERKIDZ

Lily's Passport to Paris
Copyright © 2008 by Women of Faith

Requests for information should be addressed to:
Zonderkidz, 5300 Patterson Ave SE, Grand Rapids, Michigan 49530

ISBN 978-0-310-70555-0

Published in association with the literary agency of Alive Communications,
Inc., 7680 Goddard Street, Suite 200, Colorado Springs, CO 80920.
www.alivecommunications.com

Editor: *Barbara J. Scott*
Cover design: *Jody Langley*
Interior design: *Amy Lengeeler*

Printed in the United States of America

One

*U*h, Lil," Lily Robbins' mom said from the back door. "You've picked a strange time to garden, hon." She glanced at her watch. "Our train leaves in an hour and a half."

Lily tried not to give her mom the *I-am-so-not-gardening-right-now-Mother* look and instead held up the plastic Ziploc bag she'd just filled with Oxford soil.

"I'm just getting some dirt to leave in Paris," she said.

One corner of Mom's lips twitched into her almost-smile. "Don't they have enough there?"

Again Lily controlled her face, and she smothered a sigh too, just to be on the safe side of attitude.

"It's a spiritual thing. Mudda told me I should do it."

"I definitely wouldn't question your grandmother—bizarre as the woman can be sometimes." Mom blinked. "Did I say that?"

"Nobody'll ever hear it from me," Lily said. She got to her feet and brushed the dirt from the knees of her jeans—or at least, she tried to. English spring dirt was practically mud, and it stuck to denim like Elmer's Glue.

"I hope you didn't pack all your clean clothes." Mom's mouth was twitching again. "I'm assuming you're all packed."

"I am."

"How many journals did you cram in there?"

Lily couldn't stifle the sigh this time. "Only two—in my suitcase."

"And in your backpack?"

"One. But I need them, Mom!"

"And you're going to need a chiropractor too." But before Mom could say more—and Lily was sure there was more—there was a yell from inside the house that turned Mom immediately on her heel. When Lily's adopted ten-year-old sister, Tessa, let out a bloodcurdling scream like that, she was either winding up to belt Joe or getting ready to hurl some frustrating object against the wall. Lily suspected it was the suitcase Mom had told Tessa to pack.

Betcha she can't get it closed, Lily thought, as Mom disappeared inside the back door. The last time Lily had seen it, there were four inches of Tessa's belongings rising above the lid line, and she'd still been pulling stuff out of her drawers. Dad said it was because she'd been in and out of so many foster homes, she was used to taking everything she owned with her wherever she went.

And Mom's complaining about me carrying a couple of journals, Lily thought.

But she had to reconsider that as she climbed the back stairs to change her jeans. It wasn't that Mom, or Dad, or even Tessa, or Lily's brothers, Joe and Art, actually *complained* about her spiritual stuff—like keeping journals and lighting candles and dropping off and picking up dirt in their travels. It was more that they didn't *understand* it, except for Dad, and he wasn't going with them to Paris.

And neither was the only other person who "got it."

Lily squinted through the dim upstairs hall light at the clock, which was barely visible against the faded-daffodil wallpaper. She still had time to run across the street to

St. Margaret's and see Sister Benedict before Kimble and Ingram showed up to say good-bye.

She made a move toward her bedroom door to tell Mom, but she could hear her in there, coaxing Tessa in a voice that was balancing on a tightrope of patience. Not a good time to interrupt. She considered asking Dad, but he was at the bank, getting some Euros so they wouldn't have to exchange money when they first arrived in Paris.

I just got used to pounds and shillings here, Lily thought, as she headed for the boys' room. *Now it's Euros, for Pete's sake—one more reason to stay here instead of running off to France for a month.*

Lily shook her mane of red hair and with it shook off that thought and the dozen others that always followed like little cars on a toy train. *Save it for Sister Benedict,* she told herself. *She'll keep you from becoming a train wreck.*

The boys' door was ajar, and it was obvious that Joe, her eleven-year-old brother, wasn't in there, because it was as quiet as a British bank—and *that* was quiet. People in England, Lily had found, always talked in whispers around money.

But the quiet didn't mean her eighteen-year-old brother, Art, *wasn't* in there. In fact, the more deathly silent a room was, the more likely Art was occupying it, especially today. He was in one of his moods.

Lily took a deep breath, steeled herself for possible projectiles, and tapped on the door.

"What?" came the voice from within.

Lily pushed the door open and flashed a smile so forced it hurt her lips. Art didn't see it. He was lying on his back on one of the sagging twin beds. His short, curly red hair was brilliant against the dingy pillowcase, his hands folded over his chest, and his eyes closed. At least he didn't look as if he were going to pick up the bedside lamp and hurl it at her.

"Could you give Mom a message for me?" Lily said.

Art answered in a voice soaked in contempt. "If I see her."

How could you not see her? Lily thought. *She checks on you every seven seconds, for heaven's sake.* If it wasn't to make sure his blood sugar wasn't too far up or too far down, it was to try to pull him out of a black mood or make sure he wasn't about to spiral down into one.

Lily had thought more than once that it was no wonder Art got irritable. Between finding out he had a disease called diabetes and having Mom hover over him in very un-Mom-like fashion, he pretty much had a right to be cranky as far as Lily was concerned.

Lily softened a little. "I'm bummed out too," she said. "I'm sure Paris is going to be great and all that, but I've got friends here."

"Bully for you," Art said. "I've got friends back in Jersey—"

"Well, so do I—"

"Who are right now packing to go to State Finals with the jazz band *I* started," Art moaned. "One more thing I've had to give up because of this stupid disease, so don't go there with me, all right?"

He opened one blue eye just wide enough to glare at her like some kind of pirate. Lily felt all sympathy fade away.

"Sorry," she said. "Would you just tell Mom I'm going to see Sister Benedict, and I'll be back in time to leave for the train station?"

"Whatever," Art said, and let his eye slam shut again.

Lily went downstairs to the kitchen, scribbled a note to Mom, and leaned it against the goodies for the train that were stacked on the table. Somebody was bound to see it there.

It was starting to drizzle again as Lily crossed busy Woodstock Road. She pulled up the hood of her rain jacket and charged ahead. She was used to rain, cars going down the "wrong" side of the road, and everyone speaking in clipped, proper-sounding tones. Some people even told her she was starting to sound rather British herself.

But one thing that never ceased to amaze her was St. Margaret's, and all the other churches in England that she had visited, for that matter. They were so seasoned with age and holy looking, inside and out.

Lily ran her hand across the pale stone of St. Margaret's wall as she cut a corner amid the tall trees that bent over the peaked roof. She could almost feel the prayers of centuries of people who had entered before her, right there in the cold, damp stone. She always sensed them, as she did now, passing under the covered walkway where the statue of Christ looked down from his cross. Even as she pushed open the heavy door, she could hear Sister Benedict in her head, reminding her that God wasn't only in the churches.

Remember where he spoke to you in London, she would say, her eyes murky-brown with age, twinkling in her cobwebby face.

Lily *did* remember. But the churches, especially St. Margaret's, were still special places to her, filled with their holy silence. Besides, this was where she had first discovered her pilgrimage guide.

And then as if Lily had called ahead for a reservation, Sister Benedict stepped out from a row of chairs on the slate floor into the shaft of light Lily let in as she entered. The old woman smiled so that the whole cobweb of lines danced to life.

"How do you always know when I'm coming?" Lily said.

Sister Benedict cupped a gnarled hand around her ear. "You were humming? What were you humming? I don't hear so well, you know."

Ya think? Lily thought. But she just smiled at her Anglican-nun friend and tucked her arm through the frail woman's elbow draped in her gray flannel cape. Though it was spring-warm outside, there was always a chill in the church. Lily was anxious to get to Sister Benedict's cozy cell of a room where there would be an inviting cup of tea, sunlight streaming through the tiny window, and the glow of candle flames to make her feel warm.

Once they were settled in her cell, Sister Benedict looked at Lily over the top of her nose, which reminded Lily of a cone full of marbles. "So this is your last day in Oxford for a while. I trust you've a good deal of worry about that."

"It's only for a month!" Lily said, and then she sagged. "A whole month. Am I an ungrateful little creep for not being happy that I get to go to Paris?"

"Ah, Lily, love. Drink your tea and think about what you've just said. Does our good God make 'creeps'?"

Lily sipped. She could practically feel the freckles on her forehead folding as she creased it. "I guess not," she said. "It's just that, for one thing, I'll miss Dad. We're getting along again, you know, after all the stuff that happened in December. And he understands my pilgrimage too. Not that Mom's mean about it or anything. I just don't always think she exactly *gets* it, especially since she has to spend so much time worrying about Art." Lily stopped for a breath. "He's in one of his funks again."

Sister Benedict nodded. "I expect it's very difficult

for him."

"Yeah, and when it's difficult for him, it's difficult for the rest of us. It's like he can frost up an entire room just by coming in—another reason I'm not looking forward to this trip. Nobody has much fun when he's all frozen-up like that. He used to be so cool—I mean—not that I don't still love him—I mean—he's my brother, but right now it's hard to *like* him. Is that bad, you know, with him having diabetes and everything? Should I just understand him, spit spot, just like that?"

Lily dusted her hands together, and Sister Benedict chuckled in her young-sounding way.

"You are not Mary Poppins, Lily, love, and if you were, I suspect I wouldn't be able to bear being 'round you."

"Then forget her!"

Lily watched as Sister Benedict struck a match against the rough-hewn table and lit one in the line of candles that was always present there.

"A prayer for Art," the sister murmured. "Come, Holy Spirit, come."

Lily closed her eyes and whispered yes. But the prayer wouldn't stay in her head.

"It isn't just Art anyway," she said when Sister Benedict had opened her eyes again. "I know I have a better attitude about going to Paris than I did about coming here."

"Ah, yes, I remember."

"But I'm still kind of nervous about a whole new place. What if I get homesick again? What if Kimble and Ingram find new friends to replace me once I'm out of the country? What if they figure out they'd rather just be the two of them and shut me out when I come back?"

Sister Benedict blinked, lit match in hand. "I hardly know which to light a candle for first, Lily, love." She touched the flame to wicks as she named them off. "Homesick. Missing Ingram. Missing Kimble." She chuckled as she shook out the match just before it began to singe her fingertips. "I don't think we need to pray that Ingram and Kimble will not become a twosome in your absence. I should imagine it would be more likely that the queen will take up belly dancing."

Lily snickered. Maybe that was stretching her anxiety a little. With Ingram being all about the ages of castles and the dates of kings and Kimble being all about cosmetics and available blokes—boys—they probably weren't going to run off together while Lily wasn't looking.

Besides, Lily and Ingram were thirteen-looking-at-fourteen, and Kimble was a year older. The thought of dating somebody, much less teaming up for life, wasn't in the near future in Lily's mind or Ingram's. She knew that. Kimble would have said it was, but Lily knew better. A lot of what Kimble did and said was to protect herself from all the things she had to deal with at home. Dad and Mom had explained that to Lily.

She looked up from the dancing candle flames to see Sister Benedict watching her with that I-know-what-you're-thinking look on her face. Lily knew she probably did.

"It wouldn't be this hard," Lily said, "if I didn't feel like all my friends back home had fallen off the face of the earth."

"You've still not heard from Reni?"

Lily shook her head, and she could feel her heart dipping down to meet her stomach. "She hasn't emailed me in two weeks. The only person who emails me anymore is Mudda—you know, my grandmother. And she tells me stuff like 'don't forget to go barefoot once a day no matter where you are,' and 'write down one important thing that happens every day.'"

"Wise old crone, that Mudda."

"I get an email once a week from Suzy, but that's just Suzy. She probably does it like a homework assignment. Kresha doesn't have a computer, and Zooey only writes her *name* when she absolutely has to. But Reni." Lily swallowed the lump in her throat. "She's my best friend. At least, I thought she was."

Sister Benedict kept nodding as she lit another candle. Now the little cell was flooded with light, and Lily could better see the smile that always made her want to smile too, no matter what was happening. Sister Benedict's funny thin hair and the shelf her ample bosom made across her chest made Lily want to burst into guffaws sometimes. But the sister's smile brought on genuine joy. Right now, however, it was bringing tears to Lily's eyes.

"Why does everything have to change all the time?" Lily burst out. Her breath snuffed out one of the candle flames.

"Ah, Lily, love." Sister Benedict carefully picked up the matchbook and slowly relit the wick. "Change will happen whether we stay where we are or move about. That is life itself." She peered keenly at Lily, the candlelight flickering, wisdom-like, in her eyes. "Especially when one is on a pilgrimage with the Lord, as you are."

"But you're my pilgrimage guide! How am I supposed to go on without you?"

"You can't go on unless you *aren't* with me. It's time you let God be your guide." She put up her hand before Lily could even open her mouth to protest. "You know how to do that. He has shown you again and again."

Lily gnawed on a thumbnail. "I can do it *here*, because I know this place now. But everything's going to be different in France."

"Indeed it will. Different language, different food, different customs—different things you haven't even imagined. If you should feel awkward and silly, and you will, just get quiet and feel God's presence. He will show you what to do." Sister Benedict's eyes twinkled amber in the light. "Besides, it is a good thing for all of us to feel rather stupid from time to time, just to keep us humble."

Lily felt herself scowling. If this was supposed to make her feel better, it wasn't working. Her heart sunk further into the "anxiety zone" deep in her stomach. She set her tea aside.

"Then I guess I feel pretty humble right now."

"But that is the joy of it, love! There will be no dull sameness in your life. What is it Kimble says about hers?"

"It's wet," Lily said. Kimble had been instrumental in the development of Lily's slang vocabulary since she'd come to England.

"However," Sister Benedict said. She held up a knotty old finger. "It wouldn't matter if you traveled to Paris and Rome and Tokyo or stayed right here in Oxford. Once you are on such a pilgrimage as yours, you will continue to change. You are shedding that false self and finding the true soul God gave you."

"Tell me again how I'm supposed to keep finding me?" Lily said. "I know you told me a hundred million times, but right now I'm all confused again. See, that's why I need you—"

Sister Benedict put her finger to her own lips. It was, Lily knew, her kind way of saying, *Shut up, Lily.*

"You look for the sacred all around you," she said when Lily was quiet.

"And not just in the churches, right?" Lily whispered.

"Not just in the churches. Although I'm told you don't want to miss Notre Dame. Magnificent cathedral." Sister Benedict gave a nod. "Look in God's details, Lily. You will see him at work showing you what he wants you to do. That is what Jesus did. That is where you will find both God and yourself."

They both gazed for a long moment into the candles. Lily could feel herself calming down, feel her heart returning to its normal place, feel God's Spirit working within her.

And then the moment was splattered like a foot in a puddle by someone knocking enthusiastically on the door.

"Hey, Sister B—is Lily in there?"

Lily rolled her eyes. It was Tessa. *I bet I could hide in Fort Knox and she'd find a way to get in*, Lily thought. *Of course, I did leave that big old honkin' note on the table.*

Sister Benedict called to Tessa to come in, which she did with more noise than the convent halls had probably heard in centuries, Lily was sure.

"Would you shush?" Lily said.

"Okay," Tessa whispered in a voice about as soft as a foghorn. "Mom says you gotta come home—it's almost time to leave for the train station. And Dad wants to check everybody for the billionth time to make sure we all have our passport thingies." She turned then to Sister Benedict, her big green eyes glowing in the light. "We're goin' to Paris today."

"Are you now?"

"My mom's gonna show some missionary over there how to teach street kids to be physically fit and stuff like that."

"It's a fine ministry your mother has."

Tessa cocked her head of short, wavy, dark hair. "Mom's not a minister."

"Indeed she is. Everyone has a ministry, Tessa my

pet. Even you."

"That's a scary thought," Lily said. "Come on, Tess. We better go."

Tessa leaned lazily against Lily's arm. "We got some time. Just as I was leavin', Art started havin' one of those insult things."

"He insulted Mom?"

"He assaulted your mother?"

Tessa looked at both of them in disgust. "No—one of those things where he starts talking like he's drunk and gettin' the shakes, and you have to give him orange juice or somethin'."

"An *insulin* reaction!" Lily said. She turned to Sister Benedict, who still looked bewildered with her hand cupped around her ear. "When he takes his insulin medicine but doesn't eat enough, he has this weird reaction. One time Dad *and* Joe had to hold him down while Mom poured juice down his throat."

"He doesn't take care of himself like he's supposed to," Tessa said, sounding exactly like Mom.

"I think I shall keep his candle lit for a while then," Sister Benedict said. "And the rest—" She bent her head toward the candles.

"Let me put 'em out!" Tessa said. She grabbed for the snuffer and then let it clatter back to the table. "I mean, could I?"

"I wish you would."

Sister Benedict smiled and Lily cringed as Tessa pressed the snuffer's cone over each flame, gushing wax around its sides and sending smoke all over the tiny cell. But Lily knew what the smile was for. Tessa was saying the words along with the two of them: "Let the light of Jesus be in our hearts today, O God, our Father, and let it guide our way."

When the last candle was put out, Tessa looked up at the smoke-filled room and said, "That rocks."

"Amen," Sister Benedict said. "Now off with you." She gave Lily a sly smile. "Go on, now, spit spot."

If Tessa had ever even seen *Mary Poppins*, she didn't let on. She bolted out of the room with the same clatter she'd come in with. Lily turned to Sister Benedict with her chin trembling.

"No tears now, Lily, love," Sister said as she wrapped her arms around her. "Just a hug—and this."

She let Lily out of her broad-shouldered squeeze and pressed a lumpy bundle into Lily's hand.

"Put this in that pilgrimage satchel your grandmother gave you," she said. "You'll need it on the journey, I should think."

Lily fought back tears and nodded. And then there didn't seem to be anything to do but go. As she hurried through St. Margaret's, she whispered, "Here I go again, God. Please promise me you'll be there."

But she heard only the holy silence.

Two

"All right, I need to take roll call," Mom said. "Art—passport?" Art didn't answer. He just held up the little blue booklet and grunted.

"Lil—passport?"

Lily pulled her eyes away from the bevy of creamy-skinned children who were all chattering away in what she could only assume was French. Almost everyone in the airport, including the person on the intercom, was speaking in sentences that had a lilt at the end of each, a small lifting up that made her want to raise her eyebrows. But somehow it seemed doubly unusual to hear it coming from little kids.

"Yo—Lil."

"Here!"

"Do you have your passport?" Mom said.

"Yes. It's in my backpack."

"I want to see it with my own eyes. Joe?"

"Here—yeah, I got it—looky-looky."

Joe waved his passport a few inches from Mom's face. She gave him a look. "Tess?"

"I'm here. It's that blue thing, right?"

One of Mom's eyebrows went up.

"I *think* I got it—" Tessa said.

"Aw, man, tell me you didn't lose it," Joe said. "Mom, you oughta carry it for her, dude."

Mom's other eyebrow lifted. "If we ever get separated, you each need to be carrying your own passport for identification. Tess, you need to find it or you don't get past those guys in uniform." She pointed at two burly men dressed in black and white who looked as if they had long ago forgotten how to smile.

"I got it," Tessa said. She revealed her big front teeth in a grin. "I was just messin' with ya."

"Those dudes will mess with *you*," Joe said. "I saw a show once where they wrestled some guy to the ground and broke one of his arms 'cause he was jokin' about havin' a bomb in the airport."

"Don't *even* go there," Mom said. "Just show me those passports."

Both Lily and Tessa waved theirs, and the group was once again under way. Lily figured the "dudes" in the black and white uniforms must feel sorry for Mom because they didn't search any of their luggage or ask any questions. Lily was relieved.

Joe had done nothing but talk the whole way on the train from Oxford and the plane from London about shows he'd seen where security guards tortured suspected terrorists. He'd had Lily biting her nails over whether they'd think the little baggie of dirt in her suitcase was some kind of explosive.

"Wait for me just on the other side of that wall," Mom called to Art as he grabbed his suitcase off the belt. "The Edwards are meeting us there."

"Who are the Edwards again?" Tessa said.

"You got a head like a colander," Joe said. "Everything

goes right through it."

"They're that American family that lives here and helps out people on missions," Lily said.

"Will they be able to speak English?" Tessa asked.

"They're Americans, lame-o," Joe said.

Lily glanced back as the three of them pulled their suitcases off the belt. Mom was too far away to have heard that, or Lily knew she would have been all over Joe. They weren't really supposed to call each other names. But traveling seemed to bring out the worst in everyone. She sighed. This could be a long month.

They rounded the wall Mom had told Art about, and there he was, plastered against it by a rounded man and woman with smiles the size of Montana and hair the color of London fog. Lily could hear them talking far above the hum of the airport bustle.

Yikes, Lily thought. *Nobody else is that loud.*

At least there would be somebody making more noise than Tessa.

"This *has* to be the rest of your family!" the woman said as Tessa, Joe, and Lily reached Art. She put her dimpled hand to her cheek with its round splotch of blush. "What a precious little family! Bless your hearts!"

Everything about Mrs. Edwards had an exclamation point attached to it, Lily thought. Including her hair, which was swept up in the back and obviously sprayed into place. Otherwise, it was defying the law of gravity. Lily looked anxiously at Tessa. If she was true to form, she'd be saying something about that hairdo in the next seven seconds.

"Dan Edwards," the man was saying as he shook Joe's hand so hard the kid's heels came off the ground. He was grinning clown-lines into his face. "This is my wife, Betty."

Before Lily could even say hi, Betty Edwards had her arms around Lily and was squeezing the breath out of her.

"It is so *good* to have other Americans here," she said. Her peppermint breath was hot against Lily's ear. "We are just thrilled to have you."

She turned her attention to Joe, who backed up as if she were a python. Tessa leaned against Lily and whispered, "We aren't staying with *them*, are we?"

Lily just shook her head at Tessa and tried to look pleasant. Somebody had to. Joe was making no attempt to hide his disgust at Betty's gushing and hugging. Tessa was surveying Dan as if he were a suspect in a lineup. And Art, of course, was glowering until his eyebrows practically touched his chin.

"It was nice of you to meet us," Lily said.

Tessa pinched her hard on the back of the arm.

"Bless your heart—it is absolutely our joy!" Betty said. "And we've hired a limo. We knew we'd never fit all of you and your luggage into our little ol' car, and you just don't do the Metro."

"What's the Metro and why don't we do it?" Tessa asked. She sounded like she was conducting a police interrogation.

Betty and Dan wrinkled their noses in unison. "It's the subway—you know, under the ground," Betty said. She lowered her voice to a hoarse whisper. "And, bless their hearts, the people here don't wear deodorant. It gets a little—you know—" She finished the sentence by holding her nose.

"I don't wear deodorant, either," Tessa said.

Betty's wide, exclamation-point eyes popped open. Beside her, Dan's jaw was dropping.

"She's only ten," Lily said. "She doesn't need it yet."

"I don't stink," Tessa said.

To Lily's immense relief, Mom appeared just then, her hand already extended to Dan. Lily had to smother a giggle when Dan grabbed it and pumped it up and down with more enthusiasm than Mom was obviously expecting.

Tessa looked up at Lily, mouth poised for comment. Lily poked her in the ribs with her elbow to keep her from embarrassing all of them. All she said was, "Ow!"

"Are we all together then?" Betty said, after she squeezed Mom around the neck until Lily thought she would turn blue. "Bless your hearts—you must be exhausted."

"I'm not," Tessa said. "I wanna see Paris."

"You will, kiddo!" Dan spoke with his share of exclamation points too. "Betts and I are at your disposal. Any time you want a tour, all you have to do is say the word."

"Only not right now," Mom said. "All I want to do is get you kids settled."

Betty went into another wave of "bless your hearts" and led the way through the exit doors to where a long, sleek black limousine waited for them.

"Hi," Tessa said to the uniformed man who opened the trunk.

"*Bonjour, Mademoiselle*," he said.

Tessa immediately scowled. "What did you call me?"

"Mademoiselle!" Betty said. "He means you're a young lady!"

"What is he, blind?" Joe said.

Mom gave Joe *the look* and shoved him gently into the limo. Tessa was the next one to get the push. Lily followed under her own steam.

"This rocks!" Joe said as he surveyed the car's interior.

The ceiling was tufted gray velvet to match the seats, and the armrests and window frames were trimmed in silver braid. Joe was going for the button that opened the sunroof when Mom crawled in and caught him in midpush.

"Don't get used to this," she whispered. "It's definitely overkill."

"Somebody got killed?" Tessa said.

"Oh, dear, I hope not," Betty said as she slid into the seat next to Mom. "I don't keep up with such things, though I don't know how I would if I wanted to. The news on TV, the newspapers—everything is in French."

"That would make sense," Art muttered beside Lily. "Seeing how it's *France*."

Lily nodded glumly. She was feeling a little disappointed that Betty and Dan *weren't* French. If she had to be away from Oxford, at least it would be neat to be introduced to Paris by people who were actually *from* here. As the limo pulled away from the curb, Lily pressed her face to the window so she could do a self-tour. But it was hard to concentrate with Betty chattering away. Lily tried to block her out.

Paris swirled all around them. There were intersections where four and five streets came together and cars, all the size of Volkswagens, swarmed like the Beetles they resembled. People with the same creamy skin Lily had noticed in the airport streamed down the wide sidewalks past shops draped with rich colors and cafes whose tables spilled out to the curb. It seemed that every other block a large stone church with elegant spires opened its doors to the passersby.

Finally, Betty tapped on the glass and said, "Dan, tell him to turn here!"

Dan poked his head through and said, "He knows where he's going, Betts."

"Well, then, bless his heart."

"She's said that fifteen times since we left the airport,"

Joe whispered to Lily.

It didn't surprise her.

The driver turned into a street so narrow that he had to stop and back up to get the long car around the corner. The cobblestone road was lined on both sides by three-story buildings with tiny wrought-iron balconies at almost every window.

"This is it!" Betty cooed. "Isn't it precious? Now, you do have a third-story apartment. I'm so sorry for that, but we couldn't talk the man into anything lower."

"Pastor Renee said there were no other vacancies," Mom said.

"That's what he was *told*," Dan said through the window. "We think it's because you're Americans."

"What's wrong with Americans?" Tessa said.

"Nothing, my precious!" Betty said. "Aren't you just the cutest little ol' thing?"

"She definitely needs glasses," Joe mumbled.

By then, Mom was busy supervising the unloading of their stuff from the limo. Lily thought they looked like a caravan of pack mules trudging up the two flights of stairs, which climbed steeply in a spiral through narrow halls.

The walls were yellow with blue trim, which made the hallways seem cheerful in spite of their tunnel-like size. Pictures of fruit and flowers were painted right on the walls themselves. It wasn't your average graffiti, Lily decided.

By the time they made it to the top, Lily was breathing hard. Although she was used to walking everywhere in Oxford with Kimble and Ingram, she wasn't an athlete like Joe and Tessa. Neither of them had even broken a sweat. In fact, they were crowding Mom to be the first ones inside the apartment once Betty unlocked the door.

"Dude, it's *small!*" she heard Tessa say.

Joe gave an audible snort. "Small? I've seen closets bigger than this!"

"Enough, both of you," Mom said. "Follow me, and we'll find your bedrooms so I can lock you in."

"Oh!" Betty caught her breath as Lily passed her into the living room. "Well, bless their hearts."

"She's only kidding," Lily said. And then she forgot about "Betts" as she took stock of the home they would be sharing for a month.

For once, Joe and Tessa weren't exaggerating. The living room was so tiny that Art crossed it in two steps on his way to the kitchen, which she could see through the pass-through that opened onto a miniscule dining area. She calculated that the rest of the apartment was probably just as small. And since Mom, Joe, and Tessa were already exploring, she saw no point in trying to wriggle her way in too. She set her suitcase down in the living room, sat on it, and looked around.

All the furniture was very straight and made of white wood. Anything with a cushion was periwinkle blue, bright yellow, and spring-leafy green, which matched the curtains that topped the windows. There were no heavy drapes like the ones in their Oxford house—only big sets of shutters, now thrown open, covered the windows.

The white pine dining table, which would never hold the five of them, Lily was sure, was tucked under a slanted place in the wall. Art, she thought, was going to have to be careful not to bang his head getting in there. Why was the wall coming down like that anyway? The two-and-a-half step trip across the room revealed that the answer was a set of stairs.

Is that somebody else's apartment up there? Lily thought.

Or do we have two floors?

She turned around to ask Betty, but she had gone into the kitchen. Lily could hear her blessing Art's heart in there, punctuated by grunts from her brother.

I only feel a little bit guilty leaving him trapped with her, Lily thought, as she took the stairs two at a time. *It kind of serves him right for being so grumpy lately.*

The top of the stairs opened into what Lily at first thought was a closet. But there were no poles to hang clothes on, and there was a round window half covered with a crisp blue-and-white-striped curtain.

As Lily crossed to it, her toe bumped against a firm obstacle. Flailing for something to grab so she could get her balance—and finding nothing—she fell headlong onto a soft surface that smelled like her grandmother's lavender bath salts. Rolling over to sit up, she realized she was on a mattress on the floor.

"This is a futon!" she said out loud. "We slept on one of these at Suzy's slumber party!"

"Don't get too used to it, Lil," Mom said from the top of the steps. "I'm thinking I better give the loft to Art or he and Joe are going to kill each other."

"This is a loft?" Lily said. "Like the ones poets write in and stuff?"

Mom flopped down on the futon beside her and ran her hand over Lily's curls. "I know—it's perfect for you. But Art could really use the space. Maybe it'll help him figure himself out."

"If he doesn't *knock* himself out," Lily said, surveying the ceiling.

"Just try to understand, okay?" Mom said. "This is a huge adjustment for Art."

Below them, Tessa was bawling out her name. Lily

sighed.

"It's fine. She wouldn't leave me alone up here anyway."

"You're irresistible, Lil. And thanks, kiddo."

Lily caught the lip-twitch and rolled her eyes. "How long are they gonna hang out here?" she whispered.

"Only long enough for me to get the key from Betty," Mom whispered back. "So far she's hanging onto it for whatever reason."

Tessa yelled for Lily again.

"Sweet thing, there is no reason to yell in this cozy little place," Betty said below them.

"I'm lookin' for Lily," Tessa said loudly. "Li-lee!"

"Good grief, I'm coming!" Lily shouted back as she descended the steps.

Tessa, Betty, and Dan were now elbow-to-elbow in the living room. Lily suddenly felt as if she could barely breathe.

"Show me our room," she said to Tessa.

"Like you'd have such a hard time finding it."

Tessa started to squeeze between the Edwards toward the tiny hallway that apparently led to the two bedrooms, but Betty caught her in a one-armed hug. Lily cringed as her little sister's face drew down into a Tessa-scowl.

"That's one of the things that's so different here from America," Betty said. "They don't give themselves as much living space."

"And that's just the tip of the iceberg," Dan said. "You'll have a lot of adjustments here."

It was clear that being held like a pet poodle was not one of the things Tessa planned to adjust to. She wriggled away from Betty's grasp and stood behind Lily with her face in a knot as Betty and Dan went into a list.

"You'll need to watch yourselves on the sidewalks.

People walk their dogs and let them poop and never clean it up. Disgusting."

"And you have to buy your bread everyday—you can't stock up—because they don't use any preservatives—"

"Goes stale in about two hours—"

"They haven't caught up with us on that yet."

"That doesn't sound so dreadful," Lily said.

Betty cocked her head at Lily, like some strange little bird with upswept feathers, Lily thought.

"You have an English accent, sweet thing. But don't you worry—that will go away when you get back to the States."

Before Lily could protest, Dan went on as if he had to get the rest of the list out as part of his bounden duty to the Robbins family.

"The thing I miss the most is being able to zip into McDonald's whenever I want."

"They don't have McDonald's here?" Joe asked. The mere mention of the Golden Arches had apparently drawn him out of his room like a magnet. He hoisted himself up over the back of the couch, having no other route into the room except to crawl between Dan's legs. Lily was glad he hadn't opted for that.

"We've found *one*," Dan said. He held up an emphatic finger. "*One*."

"We can take them there right now, can't we, Danny?" Betts said.

"Of course! We have the car for another hour and a half." Danny roared out a laugh that jittered the vase on the shelf behind him. "Won't that be a hoot—pulling up to Mickey D's in a limo!"

"Can we, Mom?" Joe said.

Mom shook her head. "Let's save that treat for another

time. We need to get settled first."

"But they won't have the limo again! It won't be the same, dude!"

"You'll live." Mom turned to the Edwards. "We just need some time to get organized. Thank you so much for all you've done."

It took a good fifteen minutes for Mom to get the couple out of the door. It seemed to Lily that "Betts" was pretty reluctant to turn over the key to their apartment, and Lily was relieved when she finally did. She had visions of Danny and Betts popping in at odd hours to offer guided tours or something.

When the last "bless your heart" had been said and the door was closed behind them, Joe immediately wailed, "Why wouldn't you let them take us to McDonald's, Mom? That woulda rocked!"

"Because we didn't come to France to seek out American junk food. We'll go out and find a café later. In the meantime, there are suitcases to unpack."

"There's no place to put stuff," Joe said.

Tessa nodded as if she were seconding a motion to go to war. "Mom, you gotta help me—or make Lily help me."

"And then we need to go shopping for food," Mom said, waving Tessa off.

Art put his head through the pass-through. "You don't have to. That Betty woman filled up the refrigerator."

"Oh," Mom said, lips twitching. "How nice of her. Okay, let's get moving, troops. Joe, in your room. Tessa, hit that suitcase—"

"Mo-om!"

Lily put her fingers in her ears. Art pulled his head back through the pass-through. Mom held a hand up and said, "All right. That's enough."

The tiny apartment went quiet.

"We are not going to live in chaos no matter how small this place is," Mom said. "Here's how it's going to go down. Joe and Tessa will go to their rooms and unpack. And, yes, Tessa, I will help you. Art, I want you and Lily to take the instructions Pastor Renee emailed and find the mission office and let him know we've arrived. As far as I can tell, it's just a couple of blocks from here. When you get back, I will take these two out to get us something to eat while you unpack." Her lips twitched. "We might want to wait until we're settled in before we peek at what Mrs. Edwards left us."

Mom went for her bag and pulled out a piece of paper. Lily felt the butterflies coming out of their cocoons in her stomach.

"What if we get lost?" she said.

"You won't. It's too simple. Art will be with you."

"Why don't you just call the guy?" Art said.

"I tried," Mom said. "The phone is a mystery I have yet to solve."

Art had by now emerged from the kitchen, hands in his pockets, face drawn tight. Sometimes it was hard for Lily to believe this was the same brother they'd left at the Philadelphia airport eight months ago. He used to get a gleam in his eyes and do things like grab Mom and put her head in a half Nelson. It seemed like something funny was always coming out of his mouth and music was always coming out of his room.

Now he barely smiled himself, much less made anybody else smile, and Lily hadn't heard a single note from either his CD player or his saxophone. It was like living with a stranger in the house.

She and the "stranger" took Mom's instructions and

climbed wordlessly down the stairs to the street. Once out
of the little vestibule with its confusing array of doorbells
and mailboxes, Art finally said, "We go left."

Stomach butterflies, fully shed of their cocoons, batted
freely about inside Lily. She turned left as close to Art as
she dared, as if she might lose him any second. But as
she turned—she got her first real look at Paris.

Three

It was like being in a movie, Lily decided. The alley they lived on smelled like fresh-baked bread and recent rain and coffee beans.

At the café right on the first corner they came to, a man sat reading his newspaper at an outside table, a miniature coffee cup curling out steam on the round, red-topped table. When the waiter in a black vest, lounging against the wall with a tray under his arm, nodded politely at Lily, she decided she could fall in love with Paris.

A good decision, that was plain as she and Art made their way down the busier street that their alley of a road led them to. They passed an outdoor market, with bins piled high. The apples looked juicy even with their skins on, and the asparagus was so green she wanted to touch it to make sure it was real.

"Even Tessa would eat that," Lily said.

Art just grunted and consulted the directions. "We go three blocks on this street."

With only three blocks to absorb, Lily put her attention antennae up. She could hear Sister Benedict in her head telling her to look for the details. And there were so many.

Red and blue and yellow striped awnings reached out

in cheery contrast from the gray stone walls. A woman carried a French poodle as she strode past Lily on the wide sidewalk. A rose bush climbed up the wall of a garden, which she could see through a black iron gate, its blooms as big as cabbages.

A graceful display of gold and red and green coats in a shop window, so different from the neon, garish colors Lily had gotten used to in Oxford, lured her to press her nose against the glass.

It's softer here, she thought. *England is a dog—one of those kind that people brush all the time and have papers for. But France is a cat.*

She was congratulating herself for that image when Art grunted and said, "This is it."

Lily pulled her gaze from a passing dark-haired woman whose graceful neck arched like a swan's and looked in the direction Art was grunting. They were standing in front of a building with broken front steps and paint that crumbled in chunks around the doorway. A faded sign hung above it.

"Does that say this is the mission?" Lily said.

"It says it's some kind of school," Art said. "But I don't think that's what it is anymore. Burlington County would condemn this place so fast."

"Maybe this isn't the mission then."

"This is it. Mom said the school closed down and they're renting part of the building to them."

Art took the two steps up to the door, walking gingerly around the gaping cracks. Lily followed as he pushed open the thick wooden door. She could smell the age even before she stepped inside.

The smell wasn't the only thing that was old. The floor was worn down in the center, from what Lily assumed was about a hundred years of students' feet. The walls were a dingy green and bare except for the occasional tacked-up paper—which she couldn't read. This, she decided, would be a good place for some of those wall painters who had been in their apartment building.

"This is supposed to be a youth mission?" Lily whispered.

"Yeah," Art said.

"Why would any kids want to hang out here?"

"Ya got me." He squinted through the dimness at the instructions. "Office is around the next corner."

Lily trailed after him, shivering as she imagined past students looking out suspiciously from the closed class-room doors that lined the hallway. She was glad to make the turn into a section where light came out of sconces on the walls and the smell of fresh paint replaced the mustiness. There was a door open just a few feet away, and Lily recognized the name "Renee" painted in lively red letters across its foggy glass.

"This must be it," Lily whispered, though she wasn't quite sure why she couldn't let herself talk out loud.

Art had his hand almost to the doorknob when a man's voice bellowed from inside the office. The words were foreign, but his tone made anger as clear as if he were shouting in English.

Art scrunched up his face. "He sounds like a French horn."

"Maybe we should come back later." Lily edged away from the door. "This probably isn't a good time."

"Ya think?" Art said.

Even as they turned to go, a female voice bellowed back at the male one on the other side of the door, sounding every bit as angry. *One thing's for sure,* Lily thought. *She's not afraid of whoever's screaming at her. I'd be crying in a corner.*

"Major fight," Art said. "Let's go."

There was no chance to make an exit, however, because the door burst open and a skinny, middle-schoolish boy-figure bolted out into the hallway, shouting something in French. When Lily and Art both looked at him blankly, his eyes reflected a snap decision, and he hurled himself at Lily, tackling her to the ground like a middle linebacker.

"Down!" he cried in English. "Head down!"

Lily couldn't have kept her head up if she'd tried, so she guessed he was yelling at Art. She hoped Art had enough time to follow those directions, because a second later, something hard hit the floor within inches of where she lay plastered under the skinny kid who was a whole lot stronger than he looked.

"What the—?" she heard Art yell. "Get off her, man!"

"You don't understand!" the boy said.

That was obvious. Lily heard the door bang open even wider and sharp, going-somewhere-important footsteps heading right for her and Skinny Boy. He peeled himself off of Lily and pulled her by the arm out of the path of a pair of boots with heels like long pencils. Lily got up on her forearms in time to see a shiny head of light brown hair toss, as its owner shrieked yet another stream of purple-angry French toward the door.

Skinny Boy scrambled up and said something coaxing to her, but the girl, who looked about eighteen, swung her hair around again, leaving a few strands stuck to a creamy-skinned face with brown eyes that broadcast as much fury as her mouth did. Skinny Boy obviously didn't miss it because he kept quiet. But when she stomped off down the hall, he hurried after her.

Art and Lily were still frozen when he came back a

few steps and once again spoke to them in French. When neither of them answered, he looked for a moment as if he were teetering on a balance beam, and then he took off after the girl.

Art and Lily turned and stared at each other.

"What just happened?" Lily said.

Art leaned down and picked up the object that had only barely missed Lily's head—and maybe Art's too. It was a long, thin loaf of bread, the kind they always had with spaghetti back home.

"Batty Betts wasn't kidding," Art said. "This is some *stale* bread. Somebody could kill ya with this."

"I think somebody tried."

Lily got to her feet and wiggled her ankles to check for broken bones. Another form filled the doorway. Art ducked.

But the man who stood there, working a thick black mustache and matching eyebrows, was neither yelling nor brandishing a loaf of yesterday's baked goods. His dark eyes were definitely sad as he looked down the empty hallway and then turned to Art. Something French came out from under his mustache.

"*Je ne parle pas Francais,*" Art said.

Lily stared at him, even as the man burst out in English, "I am so sorry, Monsieur. Please forgive this ugly scene. It is a travesty, this."

Lily couldn't take her eyes off of the man. His *R*'s sounded like he was trying to cough up a hairball, just like all the French she had heard, but his English was more perfect than her grammar teacher's back in Burlington. And if he had been the one blaring like a French horn a few minutes before, he had had a personality transplant or something. His voice was now warm—*like a pot of tea wrapped in a cozy*, Lily thought. It was a perfect detail she was going to have to write down.

By now he and Art seemed to have sorted out that they were Madame Robbins' children, and he was the very Pastor Renee they were looking for.

"Mademoiselle Lilianna!" he said. And then to Lily's bewilderment, he grabbed her by both shoulders and proceeded to plant a kiss on each of her cheeks.

When he let go of her and went for Art, her brother stepped back and offered his hand so fast that it made Lily have to stifle a giggle.

"This is indeed an honor!" Pastor Renee said for about the fifteenth time. He was as consistent with that as Betty Edwards was with her "bless your hearts," only Lily didn't mind them a tenth as much. Pastor Renee had a face she wanted to stare at for hours, collecting every detail of the soft creases in his tawny skin, every tuft of his busy eyebrows and mop of gray-streaked hair, every expression that sprang so easily to his eyes. She hadn't even minded the cheek-kissing so much, come to think of it.

"You must come in and have a coffee," he said.

"We mostly just came to tell you we're here," Art said shrugging. "So—we're here."

"And that calls for celebration. Come, I have some pastries."

Lily followed without any further urging, though she could feel Art stiffening up behind her as they entered the office.

Too bad, Lily thought. *You can be all grumpy if you want to, but I've got details to collect. Sacred details.*

As Lily waited while Pastor Renee removed a stack of folders from a chair so she could sit down, another thought curled easily into her mind: *It feels like God in here. Pastor Renee must know him pretty well.*

She settled into the chair with its faded brocade seat and ignored the disgruntled expression on Art's face as he slouched in the one beside her. She just hoped Pastor Renee didn't get his feelings hurt because Art was only grunting answers.

Actually, Pastor Renee seemed quite happy at the moment. English flowed from his mouth as if it were on a silk ribbon while he busied himself pouring something thick and black into tiny coffee cups and prying open the lid on a white box to reveal a collection of flaky-looking rolls that made her want to drool.

When he stepped out to get cream, Lily leaned toward Art and said, "When did you learn to speak French?"

"I don't speak it," he said, as if she'd just asked him the stupidest question he could imagine. "I just took it for two years in middle school. All I remember is *je ne parle pas Francais*. That's 'I don't speak French.'"

"I gotta learn that," Lily said. "You have to teach it to me tonight."

There was a flat refusal in Art's eyes, but he didn't have a chance to voice it because Pastor Renee returned, swept some papers from his desktop, placed his little feast on it, and said to them, "Voila!"

That's really a French thing! Lily thought. *I thought they just said that in cartoons!*

Making a vow to say it at the next available opportunity, Lily accepted the cup Pastor Renee offered her. As the pastor launched into a complete description of every delicacy in the box, Lily happily took a sip. Something hot and bitter filled her mouth, and she looked around wildly for someplace to spit it out.

"It is good, Mademoiselle Lilianna?" Pastor Renee said. His eyes were bright and hopeful, almost like a child who says, "Do you like my picture?"

Lily nodded and forced herself to swallow. The next step was going to have to be to dump this cup—and warn Art. In his present mood, he was likely to spew the stuff all the way across the room.

Even though she'd downed the mouthful, the taste got more and more bitter in her mouth as the seconds ticked by. Art, she saw, had finally selected a puff of a thing, which she snatched from his hand and popped, whole, into her mouth. It melted there like a pat of butter.

Pastor Renee looked at her curiously, and she tried to smile, which only resulted in a display of partially chewed pastry dough. Her grandmother, she knew, would be having a fit.

"I see you will have to choose another, my friend," Pastor Renee said to Art.

As he offered him the box again, Lily got up and hoped she looked like she was going to gaze out the window behind the pastor's desk. There was a struggling plant on the windowsill that became the receptacle for the contents of the cup.

"Don't die," she whispered to it.

"How do you enjoy the coffee?" Pastor Renee said.

Lily whirled around, certain he'd seen the whole thing, but his smile was soft. At the same time, she saw Art about to take a large bite out of what appeared to be an éclair. Her own predicament was swept aside by something she'd forgotten until now.

"Art, you can't have that!" she burst out.

"Pardon?" said Pastor Renee.

"He can't eat that—he'll get sick! He has this disease—"

She stopped short as Art's eyes cut into her like a pair of knife blades. The only thing that saved her from being chopped down in her prime, she knew, was a timid knock on the door. Skinny Boy poked his sand-colored head in.

"Monsieur Etienne?" he said. The rest was a stream of French that had Pastor Renee nodding his head. The door opened wider, and Skinny Boy dragged High-Heeled Girl in by the arm. Lily saw Art shrink back, which she felt like doing herself, except now that she could get a better look at her, Lily wanted to study the girl.

She saw that the pretty features—the perfectly tilted nose, the pouty mouth, the cheekbones right off the cover of a teen magazine—were so hard that they seemed to have been chiseled out of marble. The boy, on the other hand, was grinning now, bringing a fine peppering of freckles to life across his nose. He appeared to be about Lily's age, maybe a little older judging from the way he was forcing High-Heeled Girl to step right up to Pastor Renee. He moved like he had years of experience with stuff like this. Lily was now cringing back like she was expecting a snake to strike. She was relieved when Art put down the éclair and moved toward the door.

"We should go," he said to Pastor Renee.

But the pastor shook his head, his eyes hard on High-Heeled Girl.

"Wait a moment, please, my friend," he said. "You are owed an apology."

"No, really, it's okay," Lily said quickly. The butterflies had already doubled in size and number.

"No, it is certainly not 'okay.'" Pastor Renee looked down at High-Heeled Girl, his eyes like two smoldering pieces of charcoal. Skinny Boy poked her in the back.

High-Heeled Girl turned slowly toward Art, who somehow managed not to crouch back like cornered prey.

"*Pardonne moi, sil vous plait*," she said in a voice that

had no expression whatsoever.

"*Merci*," Art said.

"No, no, no," Pastor Renee said. *His* voice was threatening to go back into French-horn mode. "Odette, Christophe, these are fine Christian young people. They are the children of Madame Robbins, who has come from the United States to teach you. Lilianna and Arthur deserve a sincere apology."

Lily's stomach released the butterflies up her esophagus. Odette looked as if she would rather eat that brick of bread than say another civil word.

If she even understands him, she thought. *I think he's saying all of that in English for our benefit.*

But Odette did begin to speak to Art, though it was in French, and it didn't exactly sound sincere. In fact, it sounded like one of those waitresses in Philadelphia who hates her job and acts like she wants to bite your head off when you're ordering a sandwich. Lily watched Odette dig into Art with her eyes and thought that evil Ashley Adamson back at Cedar Hills Middle School could take some how-to-scare-the-daylights-out-of-people lessons from this chick. Ashley was all about insults and rude remarks. This Odette girl had already shown she wasn't afraid to use weapons.

When, after a sharp nod in Lily's direction by Pastor Renee, Odette turned to her, Lily flashed a fake smile and said, "No, really, Odette, it was nothing. You didn't mean to hurt us—we just happened to be standing there."

The girl said nothing, at least not with her mouth. But her very brown eyes spoke clearly: *No, oh lowly one. My aim was just bad.*

"We really have to go," Art said. He jerked his eyes from Lily to the door.

Lily was more than happy to cooperate. With a short good-bye to Pastor Renee, she hurried out behind Art.

"Yikes," she whispered to him. "I've seen nicer girls on *America's Most Wanted*."

Art, of course, just grunted.

Four

Tessa met Lily and Art at the door when they got back to the apartment, face triumphant.

"We're having pizza for dinner," she said.

"That's not French!" Lily said.

"No, but it's a peacemaker." Mom wrapped the sleeves of a sweater across her chest as she pointed to the door. "Let's go. You can unpack later. Betty told me about a place just a couple blocks down."

"Then it *definitely* isn't French," Lily said.

Mom's mouth twitched. "She said we wouldn't like it because it wasn't at all American."

At least there was that, Lily thought, and she set herself to the collecting of details. Although she saw a filmy peach-colored curtain blowing from between an open pair of shutters and a window shaped like a keyhole, it was hard to concentrate. Tessa and Joe were carrying on a constant dialogue about how that Betty lady must have lied because they sure weren't finding any dog poop on the sidewalks. Their disappointment was being broadcast loud and clear along the Paris streets. Lily was relieved to see the pizzeria sign.

"Nothin' like pizza for dinner," Joe said as they arranged

themselves at a table that actually had a red-checkered tablecloth on it.

"*Le souper*," Art mumbled.

Lily was all over it. "Is that *pizza* in French?"

"No. It's *supper.*"

Mom was gazing at the menu. "I hope your French is good enough to decipher this."

"Just cheese," Tessa said. "And pepperoni. Lily likes pepperoni."

"No little fishes," Joe put in. "You know how to say those?"

"Anchovies," Art said. He looked up as the waiter approached. "Uh, *la pizza grand avec fromage et*–uh–"

The guy grinned. "You wanna large pizza with pepperoni and cheese? No problem."

"Hey!" Tessa said, pointing at the waiter. "You talked in English!"

"And better than you do, I might add." Mom's mouth twitched as she turned to the waiter. "Cokes all around too, please."

"Cokes!" Joe and Tessa were like a duet.

"It's a special treat for our first night in Paris," Mom said. "Don't expect it to be a regular thing."

"A really big one!" Joe called out to the waiter, who was by now ten feet away. Lily was glad Joe had Mom's deer-brown hair and fudge-colored eyes so he didn't look like *her.* Maybe the other people in the restaurant wouldn't realize she was related to him.

"All right, so dish," Mom said. "How did it go at Pastor Renee's?"

Lily looked nervously at Art.

He rolled his eyes. "So far I'm thinkin' the French are a pretty tough crowd."

Mom's mouth ceased to twitch. "What does that mean?"

"It wasn't all *that* bad," Lily said.

"Not if you're into projectiles and body slams."

Tessa and Joe brightened up like a pair of flashlights.

"Cool!" Joe said.

"Is a projectile what I think it is?" Tessa said.

"Hush, both of you." Mom looked soberly at Art. "What happened?"

Art gave a quick rendition of the scene at the mission. Lily thought he used way too much sarcasm and that he should have included how nice Pastor Renee was with the whole pastry thing. She was about to insert that into Art's story, but Mom was twirling the end of her ponytail in her fingers and twisting up her lips. That meant she was deep in thought and wouldn't be happy if interrupted.

"Was it really like that?" Tessa whispered to Lily.

"Yeah, but no," Lily whispered back. "He gave us chocolate éclairs and stuff."

"I wanna go over there!"

"Nobody else is going over there until I have a chance to check it out for myself," Mom said. The Cokes arrived, and she waited until the waiter was gone before she continued. "My plan was for you three younger kids to do your schoolwork over there in the mornings while I work. But I'm not sure it's going to be the best environment."

"What were ya thinkin', Mom?" Art said. "The whole mission's for street kids. You don't exactly learn which fork to use when you're living in the gutter."

"Huh?" Tessa said.

Mom put her hand up and looked at Art. "We'll see. For tomorrow morning, I'm going to need you and Lil' to supervise these two while I go over and check things out." Her eyebrow went up at Art before he could even grunt.

"It's just for tomorrow."

"Okay!" Lily said. She knew she sounded a little too enthusiastic, but Art was being grumpy enough for everybody.

The pizza was thick and wonderfully gooey with cheese—*fromage*, Lily kept saying. It apparently made Tessa's tummy very happy because she was asleep almost as soon as her head hit the pillow. Lily was glad she could skip the five hundred questions Tessa usually asked before she drifted off. She propped up some pillows next to her sister on the double bed and pulled out her talking-to-God journal. Beside it in her suitcase was the bundle from Sister Benedict.

Lily crawled across the bed, which took up the whole room, to the window where some light was peeking in around the shutters and opened them further. The April night was warm and soft, and the pale light from a street lamp at the end of the alley was just enough for Lily to see what Sister Benedict had packed up for her.

As the muslin cloth fell open, Lily felt a pang for the Sister. There were two vanilla-colored candles, a wooden box filled with matchsticks, and a miniature snuffer made of pewter. All that was missing for a chat about God was the Sister herself.

As Lily's tears threatened to fall, a slip of paper floated to the floor. Before she even picked it up, she recognized Sister Benedict's handwriting.

A prayer for your pilgrimage, she had written in plain, simple letters. *God, our Father, let this be a sacred journey, bountiful with the details of your love that point to your mission for your Lily.*

Lily situated herself on the wide windowsill, and leaning against the window frame, she closed her eyes. *God, that is my prayer,* she thought. *Please let this be a sacred journey.*

The thought, however, was cut short by a clanging sound from below. Lily leaned out to look. A shadowy figure was leaning over a trash can—a dustbin, Kimble would call it—its head so far in that all Lily could see was a back and a fanny and a pair of legs.

"What's going on?" she whispered.

Even as she spoke, the figure withdrew from the trash can, holding something Lily couldn't make out. She couldn't even tell if the person was a boy or a girl. But one thing she *could* see, and she watched in horror as it happened. The shadowy figure put its selection from the garbage can up to its lips—and ate it.

Lily put her hand to her mouth, and she couldn't move until the person had disappeared from the alley. Suddenly, Paris wasn't the city of cafés and beautiful swan-necked women and curtains blowing from windows it had been a few moments before. Now, with the clang of a trash-can lid still in her head, it was a dark and foreign place.

God? Lily said silently. *Was this really worth leaving Oxford for?*

And then it was as if God sent Sister Benedict's words right to her ears. *It's time you let God be your guide. You know how to do that. He has shown you again and again.*

"I'll try, God," Lily whispered. "But stay close, okay? Everything else is so foreign. I need someone familiar with me *all* the time."

Lily was awakened the next morning by a brisk rapping on the front door.

"*I* will get it," she heard Mom say in her no-nonsense voice. Then she heard the door bang open as only Tessa would do it and her husky voice saying, "Who are you?"

"Bonjour, mademoiselle! I am Pastor Renee Etienne."

"Are those éclairs in that box?"

"They are croissant for your *petite dejeuner.*"

"Tessa, for heaven sake, let the poor man in!"

With a vision of Tessa interrogating Pastor Renee in the hallway vivid in her head, Lily hauled herself out of bed. It was obvious there would be no more sleeping today.

Mom left shortly afterwards with Pastor Renee. Her orders were that they could have *one* croissant each—and only after they'd eaten a piece of fruit. As soon as the front door closed behind them, Tessa proclaimed that a "piece of fruit" was one slice of orange. The morning went downhill from there.

By eleven o'clock, Lily thought she would throw herself out the window and into the alley if she heard the phrase "This is boring!" one more time. Art seemed to feel the same way about her repetition of *Je ne parle pas Francais*, because his grunts were turning into growls. If Mom hadn't come home then, Lily was sure all four of them would have been duking it out in the living room—an area *much* smaller than a boxing ring.

"The mission scene is going to be swell," Mom told them. "Matter of fact, I'm taking the gruesome twosome back with me this afternoon. We're going to get an indoor soccer game going."

"Count me out," Art said.

"I never counted you in. I'm giving you and Lil the afternoon off."

An idea sprang into Lily's head. "Then I want to explore Paris!" she said. "I'll just stay around here. I could—"

"You could get yourself lost or wind up in some weirdo's lair," Mom said. "Absolutely not, Lil. Not unless Art goes with you."

Lily didn't even bother to look at her brother. He was already heading upstairs to his "cave."

"Now there *is* another option."

Lily glanced at Mom, who was watching her with a cautious look.

"What?" Lily said.

"Dan and Betty said they would be glad to give tours. Bless their hearts."

"Mo-om!"

"Fine, then stay here until I get home for dinner."

Lily felt herself sagging. The thought of sitting here listening to Art grunt from above was even more nauseating than the idea of listening to Betty gush. Besides, details were details no matter how you gathered them.

And I have to get the good Paris back in my mind, she thought. All she could think of now was the Paris where people ate out of trash cans.

"Okay," she said to Mom. "I guess you could call them."

Within ten minutes of her mother's phone conversation with the Edwards, they were at the door, round faces beaming. Lily couldn't get over how much they looked alike. Resisting the urge to ask them if they weren't really brother and sister instead of husband and wife, she climbed into their roller skate of a car. But as Dan lurched them out into traffic, all thoughts left Lily's head except that of staying alive in the backseat.

"All right, little Lily Flower," Betty said, as if they *weren't* about to be killed by the taxi Dan swerved in front of, "we thought we would do the Eiffel Tower first. Would you like that?"

She pressed her face into dimples and waited, as if she expected little Lily Flower to burst into squeals.

Lily wanted to inform Betty that her name was definitely

not Lily Flower, but she decided it would be better to be polite. Art was already trying to make the Robbins family look like the rudest people on the planet.

She got her face as close to the car window as she could and gave an occasional "uh-huh" and "oh" as Betty rattled on. It wasn't necessary to do much else since Betty had a lot to say. Things like:

"All the streets are called *Rue de Something* or *Avenue de Something*. If you're walking around, watch your pocketbook. There are purse snatchers everywhere."

"Now, you'll see artists doing paintings in the strangest places, and they'll want to paint your portrait. *Never* let them. They'll try to make you pay when they're finished, and they get right ugly when you don't."

And the one that made Lily have to chomp down on her lip: "Your mother did take my advice about the pizza, didn't she? Worst stuff I ever tasted in my life."

But all of that disappeared the moment the Eiffel Tower came into view, and Lily didn't hear another word Betty said from then until they drove over a bridge to its base.

The iron tower seemed even taller than the thousand feet Ingram had described to her in one of his mini-lectures. Its slim radio tower at its very top seemed to reach almost to the French-blue sky.

This is like the symbol for Paris, she thought as she gazed in awe. *Hardly anybody I know has ever seen this. Not Reni. Not Kimble. Not even Sister Benedict. I have to look at it for everybody.*

Ingram had told her that you make the journey to the top in three stages and from the very top you can see the whole city. She was already unbuckling her seat belt when Dan said, "What next, Betts?"

"She has to see the Arch of Triumph, don't you think?"

Dan gave a belly laugh. "It's Arc de Triomphe, Betts," he said. "You just can't get French, can you, Honey?"

And then Lily watched, bewildered, as the Eiffel Tower grew distant behind them.

I can't get out and go inside? she thought. *What's up with that?*

"Now, it *is* quite a drive from here, Lily Flower," Betty was saying. "But Dan doesn't mind, do you, Sweetie?"

"Not at all!" Dan said. And then he leaned on the horn and hollered, "Where did you learn to drive, idiot?"

"They drive terrible here," Betty told Lily.

I think he's the one who drives terrible, Lily thought.

Once again she tried to concentrate on details as Betty rattled on about some of the streets actually being named after Americans—President Kennedy and Benjamin Franklin—and how driving around in Paris always made her think of some movie with people in it Lily had never heard of.

The Seine River seemed wider than what Lily had seen of the Thames in Oxford and London, and the walls and benches along its banks begged her to come and sit on them. The buildings along the river looked like a row of palaces for as far as she could see.

And she was sure there had never been so many bridges across a river. Every one of them had its own special personality that absolutely *required* Lily's closer inspection. But she barely got a glimpse as Dan sped past everything, blasting away on his horn as they went.

The way Dan plowed through traffic, it didn't seem like a long *enough* trip to Lily. Before she could pick out even one face in a window or bin of apples in front of a shop, Betty was announcing that they were on the famous Avenue de Champs Elysees, where the "snooty rich people shop."

It truly was a magnificent display of store windows lush with elegant mannequins in even more elegant fashions, and the sidewalks were so wide they could hold ten people walking side by side, Lily was sure.

The Girlz and me and Kimble could walk with our elbows hooked together, she thought, *and still leave room for other people to pass.*

Then suddenly the avenue disappeared and they were in a tunnel.

"Don't be frightened, Lily Flower," Betty said, reaching back to pat Lily on the knee. "We'll be out of here in a minute. This is the safest way to get there so we don't have to fight that traffic circle the arch is in. There are something like ten streets going out from it—"

"Twelve," Dan said.

"Twelve."

"Worst traffic design I ever saw."

"Oh!" Betty said, as sunlight came into view. "There it is!" She pointed through the front windshield, although Lily would have had to be blind not to have seen the massive arch that towered above a ring of traffic that circled reverently below.

Dan pushed their car into the circle, and Lily figured she was going to have to absorb it all fast before they lunged off to the next attraction. With her face glued to the window, she took it in.

Although the arch was as massive as a courthouse, it seemed graceful to Lily, rising effortlessly to its 164 feet. Lily was glad Ingram had filled her in on *those* details, because Betty was too busy warning Dan about other motorists that she seemed sure were out to deliberately bring them to their deaths.

It looked clean and shiny to Lily, especially its pillars

with four huge sculptures. It was as if they were coming to life right from the bases of the columns.

Higher up were more sculptures flat against the marble, all of which looked like pictures of battles to Lily. She was studying the names carved around the very top of the arch and wondering who they were, when Dan gave his first tidbit of the day.

"See that under the arch?" he said.

Lily assumed he was talking about a raised rectangular stone structure and said, "Uh-huh."

"Tomb of the Unknown Soldiers from World War I and World War II," he said.

Betty half covered her mouth as she whispered loudly to Lily, "They copied us."

Lily thought it would be appropriate to stop and spend a moment in silence or something. But instead, Betty said, "See that eternal flame there? Some French delinquent tried to cook an omelet on it one time."

She clicked her tongue disapprovingly. Lily could almost hear Joe and Tessa saying—in perfect unison—"That rocks!" And then it rocked right out of sight as Dan blasted them down one of the avenues that radiated from the regal arch.

"Oh, now, Lily Flower, there's something I want you to see," Betty said. "Dan, pull over."

For the first time since they'd set out, Dan shot to the curb and stopped the car. Lily looked eagerly out the window. This must be something *really* special.

"You see that man in the blue uniform?" Betty said.

Lily followed her yet-again-pointing finger to a man standing near the door of a shop with wedding clothes on display. He looked every bit as royal as the guards she'd seen at Buckingham Palace.

"I see him," Lily said.

"That is a policeman."

Lily expected the next words out of her mouth to be, *Can you say "policeman"?*

"They call them *john-darms,*" Betty said. "Now that's one French word I've learned, and you should learn it too, as dangerous as this place is. You couldn't count on anyone on the street to help you if you were bleeding on the sidewalk." She shook her head. "They won't even speak to you if you say hello to them on the street. I've even tried that *bon goor* thing."

"*Bonjour?*" Lily said. Betty sounded only remotely like Pastor Renee when he said it that morning, but it made sense. "What does it mean?"

"Hello or something—I don't know, but they could at least say something back. All you get are snotty stares, as if you were some kind of alien. Bless their hearts, they just don't have any manners."

They sure look beautiful, Lily thought as she watched yet another dark-haired, pure-skinned woman glide down the sidewalk, neck arched, mouth full and ready to speak velvety French sounds. She hadn't seen a single redhead yet, and it was making her feel a little conspicuous.

"Is that un-Christian of me, Honey?" Betty was saying.

"You're just stating the facts, Betts," was Dan's reply.

Lily didn't think it was very Christian at all.

But Betty seemed reassured by Dan's answer, and the dimply smile returned to her face. "You know, our Lily Flower has been so good back there with all this driving around. Don't you think she needs a little treat?"

Dan showed his teeth in the rearview mirror. "You think you deserve one, Little Girl?"

I think I deserve a medal! Lily wanted to say. But she gave as polite a "sure" as she could muster.

"What do you think, Mama Betts? That little chocolate shop over by the guy with the vegetables?"

"I think our Flower Girl would like the bakery better. They have more choices. And healthier." She turned to Lily, hand slanted against the mouth again. "The French eat so many sweets."

The French rock! Lily thought. But she just nodded. Yikes. These people were driving her to think like Joe. That was scary.

Dan pulled up to a tiny shop with a sign that said *Boulangerie* and a glass counter that displayed more shapes of bread than Lily knew existed. Between that and the cramped-up feeling in her legs, she practically bolted from the backseat the second Dan turned off the ignition.

The counter opened up to the inside of the shop so that they could stand on the sidewalk and order. Behind it a rosy-cheeked woman in a white fluffy hat watched pleasantly as Lily devoured every morsel of bread with her eyes. It would have been impossible to choose among the plump loaves with their bursts of nuts and raisins and their cinnamon designs if she hadn't seen a cut-in-half one that appeared to have ribbons of chocolate running through it.

"Now you pick whatever you want," Betty said, sounding for all the world like she was doing an impression of Barney.

Lily pointed to the chocolate affair. "I'd like that one."

Betty leaned down to look, and then pinched the dimples into lines. "Are you sure you're allowed to have that? I know your mother only feeds you children healthy food. Though I don't know how she expects to do that here with all the butter and sauces they eat."

She clicked her tongue. Lily didn't say anything.

"Oh, come on, Betts," Dan said. "Look—she's disappointed."

"Are you? Bless your heart. All right, you have the chocolate, and it'll be our little secret." She gave what Lily was sure was supposed to be a giggle and turned to the lady behind the counter.

"THE LITTLE GIRL WILL HAVE THE BREAD WITH THE CHOCOLATE IN IT," Betty shouted at her.

Is the lady deaf? Lily thought. *Why is Betty yelling?*

"*Oui*, Madame," the woman said.

She reached a gloved hand into the case.

Betty tapped the glass with her fingernail. "THAT ONE!"

The lady's eyes turned to stone as she nodded and picked up the very loaf she'd been going for in the first place. Lily could feel her face blotching up in embarrassment.

I wish I knew how to say, 'These are not my parents,' in French, Lily thought.

When the woman turned to the back counter to cut Lily a slice, Betty nudged her and said, not very softly, "Do you see how arrogant they are? Do you know what *arrogant* means?"

Lily could barely squeeze out a yes, and only to the second question. She hoped with all her heart that the lady who was now handing her the slice of bread didn't speak English.

One bite made the whole ordeal worth it, however. The combination of bittersweet dark chocolate woven daintily into buttery bread pushed the English Jammy Dodgers into second place as her favorite dessert on earth. While Dan and Betty shouted their choices at the now stone-faced lady behind the counter, Lily squatted down to look at the little sign next to the chocolate loaf.

Pain chocolat, it read. Lily tried saying it out loud: "Pain chocolate."

"Pah ShokolA," said a soft voice above her.

Lily looked up to see the counter lady smiling down at her, eyes warm like Pastor Renee's.

"*Pah shokolA.*"

"Good. You sound like the French!"

Her accent was thick but Lily liked it and immediately hoped she sounded as cute speaking French with her English one. She exchanged smiles with the lady as she stood up and again bit into her bread.

"We'd better get you to the mission to meet Mama," Betty said, taking Lily by the arm and pointing her in the direction of the car.

When they were once again on their way, Betty quickly polished off her bread and said—with her mouth full—"Bless your heart, Lily Flower, I'm so sorry that woman embarrassed you, correcting you like that. But don't feel bad. I think French is so hard to pronounce." There was another knee pat. "But you don't really need to worry about it. Most everybody you need to talk to in Paris speaks our language, including the street children at the mission, who are taught English. It's just the way they work American tourists."

Lily didn't know what that meant, and she didn't ask, but if this day had taught her anything, it was that she saw Paris through different lenses than Betty and Dan. But Lily's hands started to sweat at the thought that Odette had probably understood her the day before when she'd said to Art, "I've seen nicer girls on *America's Most Wanted.*"

"Is there anyplace else you'd like to see today, Lily Flower?" Betty said.

Lily snapped back to attention. "You know, if it isn't too much trouble, I'd like to see a big cathedral. My friend in Oxford told me about a big one called Notre Dame. I love churches—"

"Hmm," they both said.

"It's pretty far from here," Dan said.

"Maybe another day," Betty said.

When Dan pulled up to the mission, Betty said, "I'll walk you in, but I can't stay. We have to get home so I can fix Mr. Dan's supper."

"It's okay, you go cook!" Lily said as she threw open the car door, anxious to escape. "I'll be fine, really. Thanks for the tour."

"You are so welcome! Bless your heart. You're such a good little traveler—I'd like to take you to that nice art museum. What's the name of it?"

"The Loover," Dan said. "You betcha! We'll do that!"

Lily just smiled and pretended she didn't know what to say to such a generous offer. She really *didn't* know what to say, except, *Not in a hundred million years!*

Then she held her breath until the car disappeared around the corner. Feeling as if she'd just been released from detention, an experience she'd only had to imagine until now, she ran up the steps in total disregard of the cracks and yanked at the big door. It didn't budge.

Then she remembered that Mom said the entrance the kids used was the side one, off the alley Lily had seen from Pastor Renee's window. More afraid of Betty and Dan changing their minds and returning than she was of people diving out of trash cans in the alley, she dove into it.

And as if on cue, Odette emerged from the shadows and stood directly in her path. Lily found herself looking into hard brown eyes.

Five

Odette's eyes were so riveting that Lily could only stare back, her feet rooted into the stone street. When Odette said something in French, Lily couldn't even shake her head.

But after a few more numb moments, she remembered something.

"*Je ne parle pas Francais!*" she blurted out.

The girl raised a suspicious eyebrow and said something else, which Lily was sure was insulting.

Lily plastered on a smile. "Do you speak English?"

"Oh, yes," Odette said. Her eyes glinted even in the alley's semidarkness. "I have understood every word I have ever heard you say."

Her English was hard and very American-sounding, and except for the fact that she didn't use contractions, it sounded as if she had learned it on the streets of Philadelphia. Lily felt herself going pale.

"I'm really sorry about what I said—"

Odette stopped her with her eyes, now flinty as steel. "You think you are something special. But it would take nothing"—she snapped her fingers near Lily's nose—"to show you that you are not."

She snapped her fingers three times in an arc above her head, and Lily was sure she was about to be shown. Above them, shutters banged against the side of the building, and Christophe's sand-colored head poked out.

Oh no! They're working together! Lily thought frantically. She was seriously considering taking a chance that she could run faster than Odette in her pencil-high heels, when Christophe shouted down, "Li-lee! You come back to see me!"

His English wasn't as smooth as Odette's but in a butchered kind of way, it was cute. The fact that he was completely messing up the grammar didn't seem to occur to him as he shouted with confidence, "You cannot live without me!"

Odette spat a few French words up at him, but he only grinned at Lily and called, "Wait for me!"

He disappeared from the window, and Lily looked at Odette. "Should I wait for him?"

The brown eyes narrowed into slits. "I do not care what you do, *enfant*. Except that you remember what I just said to you."

"I will," Lily said.

But that didn't seem to assure Odette. She just stood there, glaring into Lily's face. It was what Ingram would have called "disconcerting." And yet a small part of Lily was also annoyed.

Who does she think she is anyway? Lily thought. *What's she gonna do, clobber me with a loaf of pain chocolat?*

That was more of a possibility than Lily wanted to think about, so, stomach churning, she concentrated on taking a full Odette-survey. Details were details, after all.

Odette's thick, light brown hair was almost as curly as Lily's own red mane, and her lips too were what Kimble called "gorgey." She was always telling Lily the same thing about hers, and how she would *kill* to have a mouth that full, seeing how it was currently all the thing. Unlike Lily, however, Odette had only a light peppering of freckles across *her* nose, and she was about an inch shorter and more compactly built.

Still, Lily knew the girl was older than she was, just by the tough way she carried herself. Even if Ashley Adamson dressed in Odette's ultratight jeans and midriff shirt, the thirteen-year-old couldn't carry off the same attitude. Lily wanted to ask how a street kid could afford trendy clothes, but she didn't dare. The eyes were hardening into threats again.

It was obvious that Odette wasn't going to show her how un-special she was within the next ten seconds, so Lily challenged herself to look for more precise details. She found one right away: a tiny circular tattoo on Odette's left shoulder. It was so small that Lily couldn't figure out what it was a tattoo *of* without getting closer, but she was sure it wasn't a *sacred* detail.

Before she could inspect for more, Christophe burst onto the scene, breaking Odette's power stare. Lily would have sworn the girl hadn't blinked even once.

"Li-lee!" Christophe said.

Without warning, he grabbed Lily by the arms and kissed both cheeks. She could feel her face passing blotchy and going straight to total red.

"Christophe!" Odette said sharply.

"Is o-kay," he said, still grinning. "Renee introduce us."

Oh, Lily thought. *So that's how it works. You can't kiss somebody on the cheeks unless you've been properly introduced by someone else.*

It definitely made sense. You wouldn't want to go around laying your lips on perfect strangers.

She looked up to find Christophe still gurgling in her direction. "I am happy he introduce us," he said.

Odette gave a loud *harrumph* sound and marched off, high heels clicking on the stones.

Lily let out a long breath she hadn't realized she'd been holding. "I don't know what I keep doing that makes her so mad," she said.

Christophe made a noise with his lips that reminded Lily of her favorite horse at the stables back home. "She only—what is word?—ah—she jealous of your beauty."

Lily let out a laugh that echoed through the alley. Christophe sent his lip out in a pout.

"I have the feelings hurt," he said. His eyes were twinkling.

"You are such a liar."

"You must pay," Christophe said.

"Huh?"

"You come with me to the dinner—or I am hurt forever."

"What dinner?" Lily said.

He didn't answer but only pulled her by the sleeve to the mission's side door.

What met her as they walked through made Lily stop short, squealing her Nikes on the floor. It was a gymnasium with high dirty windows and netless basketball hoops, but at the moment it was serving as a supper hall. There were at least eight long tables covered in cheery yellow table-cloths with rings of flowing ribbons of all colors hanging above them from the ceiling. It was like a carnival set up in somebody's dark shabby basement, complete with about a thousand dancing-around kids.

"What's going on?" Lily said.

"Celebration!" Christophe said. Then he put some combination of fingers to his lips and gave a shrieking whistle that brought every kid in the place running. In a split second, Lily was surrounded by laughing faces giggling in French.

"Li-lee!" Christophe said with a grand wave of his arm. "Voila!"

A cheer went up that once again rendered Lily's face tomato-red, she was sure. Christophe put his hand up and brought them to silence.

"But remember—Li-lee mine."

As he thrust an emphatic thumb at his chest and the crowd gave a unanimous "Woo-oo!" Lily didn't think her face could *get* any redder.

A gong sounded from somewhere, and the fickle crowd immediately turned and streamed to the tables. Christophe wiggled his almost-invisible eyebrows at Lily and nodded for her to follow him to the head of the center table. Lily would have balked if Mom, Joe, and Tessa hadn't already been seated there. Joe took one look at Christophe hovering at Lily's elbow and immediately wrinkled his nose as if he were smelling rotten fish.

"Gross me out," he said, nodding at Christophe.

"This is Christophe," Lily said, in her most Odette-like voice. "And he speaks English."

Joe lowered his voice to a mumble. "It's still gross."

Tessa scooted her chair closer as Lily sat down and whispered, "You want me to make him stay away from you?"

"No!" Lily said, and then she covered her mouth. She hadn't meant to say it quite *that* enthusiastically. She could tell from the way Mom's mouth was twitching that it hadn't escaped her.

All through dinner, which was ham and zucchini and

some kind of rice in little round balls that melted right on Lily's tongue, Christophe never left her side. He made her taste everything, including the couscous—a grain—and when she hesitated, he hand-fed it to her. Joe pretended to be sticking his finger down his throat, and Tessa eyed Christophe like she had him under surveillance.

I don't know what their deal is, Lily thought. *He's just being friendly.*

Between dessert—strawberries tufted with whipped cream—and the activity, Christophe pointed to various objects on the table and gave Lily the French words for them. She tried to pronounce each one, though never to his total satisfaction. With each sound she made, he drew closer to her face so she could see his mouth exaggerating the 0's and feel it spitting out the R's.

Finally, she was laughing so hard that she had to quit, but not before she had *petite dejeuner, dejeuner,* and *soupeur* under her belt—breakfast, lunch, and dinner. Christophe told her those were the most important words.

Soon the kids began to get restless, chasing each other under the tables and filling their pockets with leftover bread ends. Pastor Renee called them all to attention on a portable intercom that squealed and set everyone to covering their ears.

As he talked, Christophe whispered the translation into Lily's ear. He could say the English words almost at the same time Renee was saying the French ones. That amazed Lily more than what Pastor Renee was actually saying, which was basically that the children ought to get down on their knees right now and thank God for Madame Robbins and her family—and also for the wonderful things Madame Robbins was about to do for them.

The pastor also asked the kids if today's indoor soccer

game wasn't the most fabulous thing they could imagine. And at that point, there was much cheering and whistling. Lily had to admit, she was pretty proud of Mom.

Mom herself just twitched her lips and then said, "Wait until I run you all into the ground with physical training tomorrow. You won't be yelling for me then." Lily was sure what Pastor Renee said wasn't an exact translation of that, because they still cheered.

After that, all "bajillion kids," as Tessa put it, joined in a game in which Christophe insisted that Lily be his partner. The whole thing completely confused Lily, and in spite of Christophe's English explanation, she still never got it. They ran up and down the gym hand in hand for forty-five minutes chasing a papier-mâché bird that Pastor Renee kept shooting into the air with a rubber band. Christophe assured her that their team had won thanks only to her and presented her with a piece of chocolate in a well-worn pink wrapper which she was sure had been in his pocket since he was about ten.

"You aren't actually gonna eat that are you?" Joe hissed to her when Christophe had said the last of his six good-byes.

"I will!" Tessa said.

But for some reason, Lily just smiled and tucked the candy into her own pocket. She was certain she would neither eat it nor throw it away—ever.

As Mom and the kids walked home at the end of the evening's activities, after receiving about twenty kisses each from Pastor Renee, Lily trailed a little behind the others. She didn't want to listen to Tessa and Joe badgering Mom with, "Do we *have* to let that guy kiss us so much?" Besides, she had a lot she wanted to think about.

The whole night had been somehow different from any

other evening she had ever spent, and mostly that was good. The only thing even close to bad, she decided, was the fact that when the kids talked to her, it was mostly in French, with an English "please" or "hi" or "cool" thrown in here and there. These mission kids evidently hadn't learned English as well as Christophe and Odette yet. She'd really wanted to make friends with them, but when she couldn't answer their questions or laugh at their jokes, they soon gave up and drifted away.

I'm either gonna have to learn to speak French, like tomorrow, she thought, *or I'm going to have to find some other way to let them know what I'm like so they won't hate me.* She kicked gently at a leaf on the sidewalk. *And I could sure use some friends.*

She wondered if Christophe could be considered a friend. He definitely wasn't like any other boy she had become friends with in her life. She hadn't been able to stand Shad Shifferdecker back home in Jersey for about the first three years she'd known him. Only about a year ago had he become okay in a surprising kind of way.

Then there was Ingram. When she'd first met him in Oxford, she hadn't been too crazy about him either. He'd actually grown on her, especially after she'd pretty much taught him how to be with a person without making him or her feel like a moron.

But Christophe was different. That thought occupied all her thoughts even after they got home, argued over whose turn it was in the phonebooth-sized bathroom, and crawled into their beds. Lily waited until Tessa stopped asking her, in midsentence, if she was *sure* she didn't want her to take care of that pesky Christopher person, and fell into a dead sleep. Then Lily crawled over her to the windowsill with her journal.

He's nice to me, she wrote. *He doesn't act like I have cooties or tell me I'm weird because I talk like a halfway smart person or make fun of my red hair. If it weren't for him, nobody probably would have even talked to me all night. He makes me laugh.*

Lily paused, gel pen over paper. He might just be the most important thing that had happened all day. He definitely had it all over the World's Shortest Tour of Paris. In fact, he was right up there with the pain chocolat.

He had also given her a nice detail to write down that far surpassed Odette's tattoo. She got the pen going again: *Christophe has two tiny dimples on his chin.*

She closed her journal on the pen and looked down into the dark alley. Tonight there were no shadowy figures digging through the garbage. But the silhouettes of the bins made her wonder if Christophe, when he was a street kid, had ever been forced to paw through trash for his *petite dejeuner.*

She closed her eyes and prayed that he hadn't.

Six

Over the next few days, Mom tried to get a routine established. As far as Lily was concerned, it was like trying to fold the four flaps of a box top when the box was stuffed too full.

In the first place, it became obvious after the first day Mom took Tessa, Joe, and Lily to the mission to do their homeschool studies while she worked with Pastor Renee that Tessa could work independently for about five minutes. After that, she was off to the kitchen, where Pastor Renee's wife, Veronique, and some volunteers were fixing lunch for the street kids—or Pastor Renee's office where a secretary who spoke no English was trying to make sense of all his piles—or anywhere else in the mission where she could find somebody to talk to, whether she understood them or not.

It drove Mom nuts, but it made sense to Lily.

"After all, Mom," Lily told her one day when Tessa had disappeared from their study room for the sixth time, "she was practically a street kid herself before we adopted her. She feels at home here."

"She's going to be out on the street again if she's not careful." Mom's lips were only twitching a little bit.

Joe, unlike Tessa, got all his work done in the first hour every day, and then *he* took off looking for somebody to play with. He'd do just about anything with anybody to fight his boredom—as long as it involved a ball. That might be basketball with the seventy-year-old janitor, soccer using a teddy bear with a volunteer's five-year-old daughter, or something called *pétanque* involving a bunch of aluminum balls and one little green ball with any kid he could scare up who was brave enough to show up in the gym during school hours.

Pastor Renee gave a ten-minute lecture to anybody who skipped the school for "poor kids," as Tessa called it, which was run by another mission in the same building. Lily wondered if that was what Pastor Renee had been yelling at Odette about the day they'd arrived.

And then there was Art. *To put it simply,* Lily wrote in her journal, *he just doesn't want to leave the apartment.* Not only that, he slept most of the day, emptied the refrigerator and pantry of any and all junk food while the family was gone, and then skipped breakfast and the supper Mom fixed.

"Your blood sugar is completely haywire again," Lily heard Mom say up in the loft one night. He was having an insulin reaction, which meant he had to have juice or chocolate or something else with sugar. "Do you want to end up in the hospital?"

"Yeah, Mom, that's really my goal," was his answer.

Mom lowered her voice—always a sign that she had *had* it. No Robbins kid was allowed to talk to a Robbins parent that way. Lily couldn't hear the rest, but she hoped Mom got him straightened out soon.

Not only did she miss the old Art, but the new Art was messing everything up. Mom said she wanted to take all four kids out to see different sectors of Paris right after lunch every day until it was time for the mission kids to show up at around 3:00 for their physical fitness activities. But Art wouldn't go, and Mom said she was concerned about leaving him alone too much or they might come back and find him in a coma. Lily had caught enough reruns of *ER* to know that wasn't good.

That meant Joe, Tessa, and Lily spent several endless afternoons watching TV they couldn't understand while Mom was up in the loft talking to Art.

"I bet she's said every word there is to him by now," Tessa said on the third day of *Gilligan's Island* in French. And then she started a food fight with Joe that brought Mom down the steps yelling, "That's it! I'm calling Dan and Betty."

Joe and Tessa looked as if they'd just been shot.

"You're making us go over there to live?" Tessa said.

"No, Lame-o," Joe said. Then he puckered his brow at Mom. "You aren't, are you?"

"No, I'm taking them up on their offer to do the sights with you kids."

"I did that already!" Lily said. She hoped she looked generous as she added, "Why don't you just let Joe and Tessa have a turn?"

"Those people are weird," Tessa said.

But to Lily's surprise, Tessa went and got her backpack without much more of a fuss, and Joe didn't protest at all, even when Mom insisted on seeing their passports going into their packs with her own eyes.

They are bored, Lily thought. She was glad she hadn't given a detailed account of her afternoon with the Edwards, or Mom would have had to send them off in handcuffs or something.

When they were packed off with Bless-Your-Heart Betty and Dan, Mom told Lily she was taking Art to Pastor Renee for "a talk."

"It's counseling, isn't it?" Lily said.

"Yes, but if you say a word to him, I'm sending you with the Edwards tomorrow."

Lily clamped her lips together, and then opened them again. "Can I go with you over to the mission? I gotta get out of here."

"By all means. I never worry about you getting into trouble, Lil."

She paused in putting on her sweater long enough to tug at one of Lily's curls. "You're the only one keeping me sane in this family right now. That's a scary thought, isn't it?"

Lily liked the idea of being Mom's sanity. It kept her smiling all the way to the mission. Then the office door closed behind Pastor Renee and a very sullen Art. Mom went into another closet of a room to catch up on paperwork. And suddenly, it was lonely. Mom invited Lily to help, which she pretended to actually consider for a second and then told Mom she was going to sit out on the front steps.

She pulled a notepad and pen out of her backpack and tucked them into her sweatshirt pocket before she slipped out the front door. There was a splash of sunlight for her to settle herself into on the steps, which she did before looking around for details.

It was lunchtime, which meant that for the next three hours, most people were someplace eating couscous or taking a nap, as far as Lily could figure out. It also meant that aside from a couple of pigeons pecking at litter, there weren't a whole lot of details to be observed.

Until a now-familiar voice called from across the

street: "Li-lee! You wait for me!"

Lily looked up in time to see Christophe dart toward her, scattering indignant pigeons in all directions. She found herself tucking her hair behind her ears and fighting back the blush that was already creeping up her neck.

"You are sad, Li-lee?" Christophe was parking himself on the step beside her and peering closely. His eyes drooped sympathetically at the corners.

"No," Lily said. "I'm just bored, I guess."

"That cannot be!"

Christophe bounced up again and put out his hand. Lily looked at it blankly.

"Come!" he said. "We go."

"Where?"

"To see Paris!"

He pronounced it, Pa-ree, with the R coming from his throat in that coughing-up-a-hair-ball way she was starting to like. As Christophe stood there grinning down at her, his hand still stretched out expectantly, Lily could fully picture the two of them dashing along the Seine or racing across six lanes of traffic to the Arc de Triomphe or gazing at all of "Pa-ree" from the top of the Eiffel Tower.

But she had to shake her head. What she *couldn't* envision was Mom saying yes to the idea.

Christophe squatted down and shook his head.

"Do not be afrightened. My sister—pah." He waved off the sister as if she were a puff of unwelcome smoke from a cigarette.

"Your sister?" Lily said. "Why would I be afraid of her? I never even met her."

Christophe made a narrow-eyed face that suddenly looked familiar.

"Odette is your sister?" Lily said.

He nodded.

Lily mentally smacked herself in the forehead. *Well, du-uh. They're together all the time.*

Her heart started to sink. Maybe Christophe wasn't so cool after all. How could he be and have the same parents as the Evil Odette?

Another mental smack. *Get a clue, girl. You and Joe have the same parents, don't you?*

Christophe reached over and tapped her lightly on the temple. "You talk to Li-lee in here?"

Lily had to laugh. "Yeah. I don't have anybody else to talk to."

Christophe pretended to pout, the way he had the night of the dinner. The chin dimples appeared.

"I am no anybody?" he said.

"Oh, I didn't mean that!"

"Then we go—see Paris."

Once again the hand came out, and Lily felt herself sag as she looked at it. She really wanted to go. She would have wanted to go if his sister had been Cruella DeVille.

"My mom won't let me," she said.

Christophe raised his eyebrow, looking comically like Lily's old English teacher back at Cedar Hills Middle School. But before she could even laugh, he was through the front door and inside the mission. When Lily caught up with him, he was already at the gym, where Mom was dribbling a basketball with three thin-looking boy-kids who obviously weren't interested in school today.

"Madame!" Christophe called.

Mom glanced over her shoulder. "What's up, Christophe?"

She caught the ball in the blond boy's mid-dribble and bounced it behind her back.

"I want take Li-lee to see my Paris."

"Can't hear you, Pal ..."

The kid with the shaved head snatched the ball out of her hands and ran toward the basket.

"That is *so* traveling!" Mom said. She groped for the whistle that was hanging around her neck.

Christophe shrugged his shoulders and leaped across the court. He grabbed the ball from Shaved Head and bounced it past him and Blond Boy on the way back down the court. The third boy, a dark-haired kid wearing a T-shirt two sizes too small, jumped up and down, waving his arms at Christophe, who ignored him and proceeded to dribble the ball in a circle around Mom.

Lily knew Mom could have had the thing so fast Christophe would still have been thinking he was dribbling ten seconds after the ball was gone. But she lazily guarded him with her arms and said, "What was it you wanted, Christophe?"

"I want show Li-lee my Paris."

"How big is it?" she said. Her eyes moved past Christophe where Shaved Head was sneaking up behind Blond Boy like he was stalking prey. She took the ball easily from Christophe and delivered it close to Shaved Head's left ear. As he and Blond Boy both dove for it with Little T-shirt piling on, Mom turned back to Christophe, running backward.

"Stay within a few blocks of the mission and be back before dark," she said. "You hear me, Lil?"

Lily could only nod in amazement. Then Mom blew the whistle at the puppy pile on the floor, and Christophe nodded gleefully toward the door.

"We go!" he said.

They both squealed their sneakers across the gym floor.

"You have see my market?" Christophe said when they hit the alley.

"Your market?" Lily said.

But he already had her by the wrist and was dragging her to the street and around the corner. A grocery with outside bins and a teal blue awning came into view. Lily didn't tell Christophe she'd passed it several times, because it really did seem like a different place with Christophe picking up three oranges and juggling them for her, and then fingering a banana as if it were a flute.

"You're gonna get us in trouble!" Lily said through her grins.

Christophe looked about as concerned as one of the pigeons. Then quite suddenly, he grabbed her arm again and pulled her across the street where two boys who looked a little older than Lily and Christophe were sitting astride a pair of parked motorcycles, amid a sea of bicycles and motorized scooters.

Christophe rattled off something to them in French, all the while gesturing toward Lily. Neither one of them seemed to be paying much attention to Christophe as they looked at her with more interest than Joe or Art had their whole lives. One of them suddenly took Lily's hand and kissed it.

Lily let out a gasp, but Christophe nodded at her. "Is o-kay. I tell him who you are."

"America!" Hand Kisser said. "I am pleased to meet you."

"Oh," Lily said. "Um—*je ne parle pas Francais.*"

She might as well have just delivered Napoleon's farewell address to them in French. They acted that impressed. The second guy, who was wearing a black jacket that hung halfway off his shoulders in the front, openly stared at her, working his way from her hair down to her Nikes.

Yikes, Lily thought. *This feels a little creepy.*

She hugged her arms across her sweatshirt and took

a step backward.

A hissing sound came from between Christophe's teeth, and he tugged at Lily's sleeve.

"We go," he said. She was surprised to see him glaring at Black Jacket over his shoulder even as they continued down the sidewalk.

"Do no be afrightened," he said to Lily.

"Is he your brother?" Lily said.

Christophe laughed into the Paris air and then pointed up, bounding on his toes like a kindergartner. "See, Li-lee!"

Lily looked up to see a nine-story building that took up an entire block. Out of every window hung either an inflated beach toy or a kiddie pool. The whole side of the building looked like a day at the Jersey Shore.

"What is that?" Lily cried. She couldn't hold back a squeal.

"Paris store." Christophe's chin was tilted proudly. "Now—see this!"

This time—and every time after that—Lily didn't think twice when Christophe plucked at the sleeve of her sweatshirt and led her off down the block in pursuit of the next detail. With no chance to stop and jot things down and her camera back at the mission in her backpack, Lily could only hope she was going to be able to remember it all:

The lion-spitting drinking fountain where Christophe stuck his whole head in and shook it out like a dog.

The kid in the *douceur de vivre*—a small, soft park—who could walk on his hands, and then held out those same hands to admiring tourists.

The old lady watering her bright red geraniums up on her balcony, who when Christophe called up to her held up a finger for them to wait and then tossed down two tarts shaped like leaves and filled with spiced apples.

Christophe caught them with experienced hands.

Lily realized as they were licking their fingers that the shadows on the sidewalk were growing longer.

"We should be getting back," she said.

Christophe's eyes took on a gleam—the one that Lily had already begun to recognize as an indication that another "detail" was about to appear. "We go a new way," he said.

Lily had a saggy feeling as she followed him.

It's over too soon, she thought. *It feels like we just got started.*

"Well, before it's over, I have to do one thing," she said out loud.

"Pardone?" Christophe said.

Lily stopped in the middle of the sidewalk and peeled off her shoes with the toes of the opposite feet and then leaned down to whip off her socks. She hadn't brought her little baggie of dirt, but she could do this. Christophe watched in fascination, a smile spreading across his face.

"Pourquoi?" he said.

"Because I have to walk barefoot at least once a day."

Lily wasn't sure if he understood or not, but Christophe pulled off his shoes too—he wasn't wearing any socks—and said, "To the mission!"

And then he took off in the opposite direction.

"Christophe!" Lily shouted at his back. "I have to go!"

He turned, running backward the way Mom had done on the basketball court. "One thing more!"

Aw, man! Lily thought as she took off after him. *I've gotta follow him, or I am gonna be so lost!*

So she trailed him into what was the tiniest alley yet, where Christophe stopped in front of a high iron gate. Lily arrived at it almost out of breath and leaned against the bars. What she saw on the other side took the rest of her wind.

"A garden?" she said. "Here?"

She was gazing at a maze of stone paths that wound among beds of flowers and luscious bushes trimmed into balls. All of it surrounded a fountain occupied by white marble angels with faces that shimmered as if they had just returned from seeing God.

"Whose is this?" Lily said.

Christophe didn't answer. He was up at the top of the gate, hoisting himself over to the other side.

"Christophe! What are you doing?" Lily glanced frantically up and down the alley. "You're gonna get us in so much trouble!"

"Eh?" he said. His face was smooth and innocent as he slid back the inside latch and pulled the gate open just wide enough for Lily to slip through.

"I can't go in there!" Lily whispered. "That's trespassing!"

"I no know this word."

"Why not? You've understood everything else I've said!"

Christophe shrugged and, wrapping his fingers around her cuff, pulled her in.

"Is okay," he said. "I have the friends."

"I hope they're not like your little motorcycle buddies," Lily said. "That guy was creepy, Christophe."

But Christophe just nodded happily as he led her through the garden to the other side of a flowering almond tree. There, a larger gate exposed the little oasis to the street. On the stone path on the inside of the gate, a young man about Art's age stood studying an easel. He looked up and smiled when he saw them, his budding mustache curving up with his lips. He was wearing an Adidas T-shirt and had a tousle of curls that fell over his forehead.

Like the motorcycle characters, Curls watched Lily as

Christophe babbled on in French, the word "Li-lee" popping in about every other phrase. But Curls didn't make her feel creepy. In fact, he smiled when he spotted her bare feet and, with a mischievous twinkle of his brown eyes, removed his own shoes. Lily felt her shoulders relaxing. She wouldn't even have minded if *this* guy had kissed her hand.

"You are American?" he said. He was shaking his head.

"Yes, I am," Lily said. "You don't like Americans?"

"Sometimes no. But you—" Curls threw his hands out in front of him. "You do not act like a tourist."

"But I am!"

"No. It is the—hmmm—wait."

Curls closed his eyes as if he were in the deepest concentration. Lily glanced at Christophe, but he seemed unconcerned. He was poking his fingers into the paint.

"Ah!" Curls' eyes sprang open. "It is the quality of your curiosity that is different. I like that very much."

"Thanks," Lily said. She made a mental note to write that down in her journal later.

"I want to make a sketch of you."

Lily looked quickly at Curls, who was pulling Christophe's fingers out of his paint and surveying his collection of pencils. Even as she watched him, Lily could hear Betty Edwards saying, *He will want you to pay him, and he'll get right ugly when you don't.* Lily couldn't believe Curls was out to take her for her money, but since she didn't have any, it might be better not to take a chance.

"I really can't," Lily said. "I was told not to and besides"—she turned to Christophe—"we *have* to get back to the mission before it gets dark."

"Eh?" Christophe said.

"Sit here," Curls said, pointing to a low stone wall

that surrounded a patch of poppies.

"Do you guys only understand English when you feel like it?" Lily said.

They both smiled at her, and Curls wafted his arm toward the little wall.

"Okay," Lily said as she perched herself on it. "But make it quick, or I'm going to be grounded for the rest of my life."

"A sketch only," Curls said. "Though I would *love* to paint you. Such hair as I have never seen—beautiful."

That did it. Lily knew she would have sat there until Mom sent out the *gendarmes* for her if that was what it took.

Curls' pencil flew over the paper, even with Christophe hovering over his shoulder, wearing a grin as wide as a slice of watermelon. In what seemed like only minutes, he made a final stroke and said, "Voila!"

"Li-lee! It is *you!*" Christophe said.

Curls held the sketch out for Lily. She felt herself frowning at it.

"You do not like?" Curls said.

"Oh, no—it's great! It's just, I don't think it looks like me."

"No?"

Both Curls and Christophe peered at it, brows puckered. Lily studied it again too. She wasn't sure how to explain it, but the girl in the sketch looked much too old to be her. Her hair flowed over her shoulders like fountain water, and her lips didn't take up half her face as Lily knew hers did. This girl looked graceful and sure of herself.

This is how I wish I looked, she thought.

Christophe, meanwhile, was shaking his head. "You are wrong, Li-lee," he said. "She is you."

Then he took the paper from Curls' fingers and planted a soft kiss on each of the cheeks of the girl in the drawing. Lily could have sworn she heard Curls purr. She didn't need a mirror to know she was going scarlet from the neck up.

"Okay, we *have* to go, Christophe," she said. She smiled at their artist friend as she backed toward the alley gate. "Thank you."

"Please return, *cheri*," he said. "I will paint you."

"Paint now!" Christophe said.

"No."

Lily tried to make her voice stern, though between the chin dimples and the dancing eyes it was hard. She turned quickly and marched toward the gate they'd come in, sorting out in her mind which way was back toward the mission. She wanted him to know she meant business.

Christophe lagged behind as she struck out down the alley, turned the corner, and, to her relief, saw the teal awning of "his" market just a few blocks down. She knew she'd practically be able to see the mission from there.

Twice she glanced back at him, and both times he was pretending to pout, kicking at the sidewalk with his bare toe. Lily turned away before she let him see her smile and walked resolutely on, her own shoes bouncing against her back as she held them by their laces over her shoulder.

As she passed the market, though, she began to feel sad again. If the day had to be over, at least they could be walking together.

And then suddenly Christophe was there, walking backward in front of her, holding out a fistful of flowers.

She stopped. "For me?" she said.

He nodded and put them in her hand, folding her fingers around their stems with his.

"These are lilies, yes?"

Lily let out a squeal—about her fiftieth of the day, she thought—and buried her face in the blossoms. The details filled every sense—the softness of the petals against her lips, the sweet, sweet smell—

The sharp bark of a man's voice.

Startled, Lily looked up just in time to see a gendarme grab Christophe by the collar.

Seven

Everything in Lily came to a halt. Her heart stopped beating, her breathing choked, and even her thoughts froze. As she stood staring at the blue-uniformed policeman who gave Christophe a shake by the back of his shirt with every question he shouted into his face, she was sure she knew what it felt like to be a corpse.

And then the gendarme turned to her, and everything began to work all too well. She thought her heart would pound right out of her chest when his voice demanded something of her in French.

All she could do was shake her head. Her one French phrase refused to take shape, and she said in quaking English, "I don't speak French. Please, I don't understand."

"So—you are an American," the gendarme said.

Lily would have been relieved if he hadn't made it sound as if that were a crime in itself.

"Your passport, please, mademoiselle," he said.

"My passport?"

"Yes, mademoiselle. You have it?"

"Yes! Oh—no!"

Lily closed her eyes, the vision of her backpack slumped in a corner of Mom's office at the mission—with her passport in it—taunting her.

"Yes—or no?" the gendarme said. His voice sharpened impatiently.

Lily could barely squeeze her own voice out. "I have it, but not with me. It's back at the place where my mother works."

"I will go! I will get passport!"

Until now, Christophe had dangled quietly in the gendarme's grasp. The officer glared at him and gave him another shake.

Lily cringed. She didn't know which was worse, the gendarme yelling at her or his flapping Christophe around like he was a dirty rug. Lily bit down on her finger to keep from bursting out into very loud crying as the policeman turned Christophe to face him, took him by both shoulders, and began a brand-new tirade inches from Christophe's nose. Or maybe it was to keep from throwing up, she wasn't quite sure. The whole scene was making her sick to her stomach.

Finally, the gendarme stopped yelling and gave Christophe a shove down the sidewalk.

"Are you taking him to jail?" Lily said.

He shook his head and snatched the bouquet of lilies out of her hand. Bewildered, Lily watched him deposit them into Christophe's open palm. She didn't have the nerve to ask any more questions as the gendarme gave Christophe yet another shove and sent him in the direction of the market. Christophe straightened his shoulders and made it the rest of the way on his own.

As the three of them stopped in front of the grocery, the gendarme called out something, and an old woman, bent over in midback, hobbled out from inside. She smiled when she saw Christophe, but the gendarme took care of wiping that off as he yapped out some long explanation.

He's the first person I've heard who can make French sound ugly, Lily thought.

By now the old woman was looking somewhat sadly at Christophe. Although the gendarme looked as if he were going to give one of his signature shoves, Christophe stepped forward, placed the flowers gravely into her withered old hands, and spoke softly to her. His head bowed as if he were confessing to a murder.

Lily held what breath she still had left as Christophe finished what she assumed was his apology. If the old woman was as angry as Mr. Policeman, Christophe was in for it in stereo.

But the market lady only made a clicking noise with her tongue and shook a knotty finger at Christophe. Her eyes were smiling, especially when Christophe leaned over and ever so gently placed a kiss on each of her wrinkled old cheeks. She immediately looked ten years younger.

Now she looks about eighty, Lily thought.

The gendarme asked her a sharp question, but the market lady didn't cower. She just shrugged and shuffled back into her store, muttering happily to herself. The policeman glowered down at Christophe and then thrust his thumb in the direction of the mission. Christophe grabbed Lily's hand, and they both scampered down the sidewalk like squirrels.

Once they were around the corner, Lily skidded to a stop and shook Christophe's hand away.

"You stole those flowers from that lady's market, didn't you?" she said. Her voice was shaking, just like the rest of her.

"I no understand—"

"Yes, you do, Christophe—you know you do!"

Christophe cocked his head like a freckled bird. "I want give flowers to you, Li-lee."

"I don't want stolen flowers! Good grief!" She folded her arms across her chest so he wouldn't see her hands shaking. "I can't hang around with you anymore."

"Only because I steal flowers?"

"Only? Where I come from, they put kids in jail for stuff like that!"

Christophe looked down at his still bare feet, his face long. This time Lily was pretty sure he wasn't pretending. "I want present for you, Li-lee, and I have no money."

"You didn't have to get me a present—not that way. You took from that lady that likes you. What's that about?"

"She knows. She is the friend."

Lily could only stare at him. *He doesn't even think he did anything wrong,* she thought.

He was watching her now, looking as if he were suffering from a toothache. His face was pinched, and there wasn't a dimple in sight. He hadn't been afraid of the gendarme or the market lady, but he sure seemed to be scared of her.

"So, do you go to the mission all the time?" Lily said.

He nodded.

"Does Pastor Renee ever talk to you guys about God? You know, about Jesus and what he taught?"

Christophe's eyes seemed to grow darker. His eyebrows drew together.

"What?" Lily said. "What's wrong?"

"Church," Christophe said. It sounded like he was spewing a hairball. "Is not for me anymore."

"Oh," Lily said. She wasn't quite sure what to say next. What had seemed so clear just minutes before was now swirling around somewhere in murky waters. This was all too confusing.

"You are angry with me, Li-lee?" Christophe said.

Actually, she wasn't. *I oughta be,* she thought. *He about got me thrown in jail!* But he didn't even know he'd done a bad thing. He seemed almost too good to *be* bad.

I'm going nuts, she thought.

She sighed. "Okay, here's the deal."

"I like the deal!"

"You haven't even heard it yet. I will still be your friend, *but* you have to *swear* not to steal ever, ever again. Not for me. Not for anybody. You got that?"

The smile that spread across his face was so real that Lily felt a pang. As they walked on to the mission in the almost-dark, she tried to at least get her thoughts into piles. She couldn't face Mom with confusion plastered all over her.

One thing she was sure of by the time they reached the side door to the mission: she could help Christophe learn the difference between the right of giving somebody a gift and the wrong of stealing the gift to be given.

I could be a good influence on him, she told herself. *This could be why I'm in Paris!*

Christophe opened the door for her, and then he stopped her with a hand on her sleeve.

"You will tell Madame Robbins?"

"Are you kidding? She'll know the minute she looks at me that *something* happened. You don't lie to my mom." Lily narrowed her eyes at him. "You don't lie to anybody."

To her surprise, Christophe nodded soberly. "That is like my mother. Once."

"Hey, Christophe!" Mom called from across the gym. "Let's go—front and center. You aren't getting out of P.T. again."

Christophe grinned at her, grinned at Lily, grinned at the world. She watched him join the group on the gym floor and felt another pang.

Lily decided to tell Mom about the gendarme incident the minute they were alone together. It wasn't the kind of thing she wanted to share with Tessa or Joe.

But the minute never happened. When Dan and Betty dropped them off at the mission just before it was time to go home, the kids were so mad their faces were purple.

"I think they had a good time, bless their hearts," Betty said to Mom.

"A good time?" Joe said as they were walking home later. "What's her idea of a 'good time'?"

"Sittin' in the back of that stinkin' car the whole day lookin' at buildings!" Tessa said.

"And listening to that Dan guy talk."

"He never shuts up," Tessa said. "I mean—*not ever!*"

"Sounds like somebody else I know," Mom said.

"No, man, that dude talks more than Tessa any day—and about dumb stuff."

"Such as?" Mom said.

If Lily wasn't mistaken, she was enjoying this.

"It was like he was givin' a lecture or somethin'." Joe walked backward to give Mom the full effect.

There's a lot of that going on today, Lily thought.

"He talked for like an hour about how we shouldn't go in the Metro—"

"That's like the subway," Tessa put in.

"—because it's dangerous and we'll get mugged or murdered or somethin'."

"And then he said the fruit at those grocery store places—we shouldn't eat it because it sits outside all day."

"Oh, and get this—he wouldn't shut up about the

unisex toilets."

"Unisex toilets?" Lily said.

"Yeah, around here you go in the bathroom at like a restaurant or somethin' and it's not one bathroom for women and one for men—everybody goes in the same one."

"Only not at the same time," Tessa said. She rolled her eyes. "That was interesting the first time he said it. But he had to say it about forty times."

"She's not exaggerating either," Joe said. "Dude, I'd rather hang around the mission than go on any more sightseeing tours with them."

Tessa nodded and eyed Mom. Lily knew if Mom said they had to, there was going to be a fit pitched right here in their alley.

"I think we've about worn them out anyway," Mom said. "I'm off tomorrow—I told Pastor Renee Saturdays were going to be our family days. We're all going out together tomorrow."

"Even Art?" Lily said.

"Yes. Even if I have to rope and tie him."

"Dude, that sounds cool!" Joe said.

Tessa put up a hand and they high-fived.

I'm glad to see you two have bonded, Lily thought. It made her feel a little bit lonely. What if Mom didn't let her hang out with Christophe after she told her what had happened?

I still have to tell her, Lily thought. *Or it'll drive me crazy. So much for being Mom's sane one.*

But there was no chance between the time they got home and bedtime. Mom spread out all the books and pamphlets about Paris they'd collected and told them each to pick one thing they wanted to see the next day.

"Your father did that when he took you to London,

right?" she said.

"That rocked!" Tessa said.

"Then go for it," Mom said.

She produced a bag of assorted pastries and made some hot chocolate with real chocolate, not the powdered kind in packets, and they all pored through the materials like they were looking for treasure. All but Art. He barely gave the stuff a glance before he went back to the loft.

I hope he's not gonna spoil the whole day, Lily thought. It had been so nice not to have his gloom hanging over her all afternoon.

By the next morning, Mom had the game plan worked out from the choices everybody had made. As they strapped on their backpacks, Lily checking at least ten times to make sure she had her passport, Mom said, "In case you get separated from the rest of us, all you have to do is find a gendarme, tell him our street, and he'll help you get home. I understand they're very nice here."

Wrong! Lily thought. The gendarme story was starting to weigh on her. She hoped she and Mom would have a chance to talk soon.

"Everybody got everything?" Mom was saying. "Passports? Cameras? Do I even have *my* camera? Oh—rats, I left it at the mission."

"I'll take pictures for you with my camera," Tessa said.

"And everybody's heads'll be cut off, guaranteed," Joe said.

Tessa punched him in the arm.

So much for bonding, Lily thought.

"We'll just go by there on our way," Mom said.

"We're not stayin', are we?" Tessa said. "I wanna go to the top of the Eiffel Tower—I mean *all* the way to the top."

"You said that eight hundred times," Joe said.

They argued that point all the way to the mission and while they waited outside for Mom to go in and retrieve her camera. Lily was about to scream for them to stop or she would start pulling their nose hairs out with tweezers when suddenly Christophe was there.

"Li-lee! Tessa and Jo-seph!"

"It's 'Joe,' dude." Joe bared his teeth as if the next step would be to take a bite out of Christophe's arm.

"Hello! Rude!" Lily said to him.

"Hey, Christopher," Tessa said. "Do you love Lily or something?"

"Tessa—chill."

They all turned to look at Art, since those *were* the first words he'd spoken all day.

"I tell you who I love," Christophe said. "I love Madame Mom."

He flashed his big grin at the top of the steps where Mom had just stepped out. Lily expected her to twitch her lips at him, but she was looking strangely somber.

"What's up?" Art said.

"I could have sworn I left my camera here," she said, "but it wasn't where I thought I put it."

"Does that mean we don't get to go?" Tessa said. Her green eyes were already headed for a fit.

"You can use my camera, Mom," Lily said. She pulled it out of her backpack and handed it over.

"Thanks, Lil," Mom said. She still seemed preoccupied as she dropped the camera into her own pack, until her eyes lit on Christophe. Then it was as if she couldn't keep from grinning.

Lily felt a guilty pang. *He has that effect on everybody but policemen. I hope she still thinks he's adorable after I tell her he used to be a thief.*

"So what are you doing today, Christophe?" Mom was saying.

Christophe stroked his chin with his fingers. "I think—study. I will study."

"Right. And I'm the Easter Bunny," Joe said.

"Eh?" Christophe said.

For once, Lily was sure he really didn't understand.

"Why don't you come with us?" Mom said. She twitched a lip in Lily's direction. "I haven't heard the specifics yet, but I bet you're a great tour guide."

Lily felt her pulse pick up. When Christophe nodded and grinned even bigger, she did too.

"Where we go first, Madame?" Christophe said with exaggerated drama.

Tessa and Joe rolled their eyes at each other—but that stopped the minute Christophe suggested they take the Metro to the Eiffel Tower.

By the time Christophe led them down into the Metro tunnel, on and off the train, and all the way up the Eiffel Tower—where Lily matched Tessa squeal for squeal—Tessa and Joe were very obviously sold on Christophe. Joe started calling him Chris, and Tessa stopped squinting her eyes at him.

From there, nobody nagged or whined or complained of boredom. Lily watched in delight as her whole family followed Christophe like the kids from Hamlin after the Pied Piper.

For Joe, they went into the Catacombes, where the bones emptied from Paris cemeteries were stored in stone tunnels. Lily said, "gross me out and make me icky!" so many times, she had Christophe saying it before they were done. "Chris" told Joe they could also go to La Conciergerie, where they used to torture people. Mom squashed that idea.

For Mom, they checked out the bookstalls along the Seine River so she could find a present for Dad. There were so many booths that it seemed like going to the fair. Lily was gathering details by the basketful.

Lily wanted to see Notre Dame, but once again, Christophe's face clouded over. So she quickly changed her mind and settled for her second choice, the Musée Grévin, where the figures of people they were studying—like Louis XVI and Marie Antoinette—were displayed in very real-looking wax scenes. Tessa and Joe complained until they realized it included everyone from Charlie Chaplin to Michael Jordan.

They were boarding a bus after that—well toward *soupeur* time, Lily reminded herself—when she realized something.

"We haven't done your thing yet, Art," she said.

Mom nodded. "I don't even know what it is—you never said."

"I bet you didn't even pick anything, did you?" Tessa said.

"I picked something."

They all leaned toward Art until Lily was sure the bus would tip over.

"And that is?" Mom said.

"I want to see the Granier Opera House."

"Goody," Joe said.

Mom gave him the look. "There will be none of that. Nobody complained when we spent an hour looking at dead bones."

"Yeah, but the opera—"

"We get off here," Christophe said.

Before even Joe could protest, he was leading them off the bus and onto a wide, busy boulevard. Mom gathered them into a group and looked around.

"I tell you what," she said. "I see a café over there.

Whoever wants to can sit with me and have a drink and a snack. Whoever wants to go with Art to see the opera house can do that. Fair enough?"

"Grenadine in Perrier," Christophe said. "You must try."

"Sounds disgusting," Tessa said.

Mom, Tessa, and Joe followed Christophe to the small tables of the café. Art looked up from his map.

"What are you doing?" he said to Lily.

"I think I'll go with you."

"Why?"

"I want more details."

"Whatever," Art said.

But his voice didn't have the edge in it that said, *You, like everything else in life, are grit between my teeth right now.*

In fact, as she practically broke into a run to keep up with his long-legged stride, she noticed that he actually seemed eager to see this opera house.

And when they rounded the corner, she could see why.

Eight

The opera house was more like a vision than a building. Lily had thought up a lot of mind-pictures in her time, but she knew that this was more splendid than anything even she could have imagined.

That Charles Whatever-His-Name-Is, Lily thought as she gazed, open-mouthed, *he must have gone to heaven and seen it and then come back to build this.*

His creation was immense and grand, with arches on the ground floor and columns on the next. Above that there was a layer of statues and carvings, topped by a frosting-like trim of gold that pulled the eye up to a green zinc dome, the resting place for three statues in flowing robes of stone. The one on top held up a gold lyre that sparkled even in the fading afternoon sun. Two more threesome statues flanked the dome. Both were so bright with the precious metal that Lily was sure the angel in the center of each one had just come from God, and his shine was still on her. All of them, Lily was sure, were alive and any minute would start one big shimmering dance right there on the dome.

The magnificence went on and on. Smaller marble pillars stood behind the massive columns on the second level, topped with gold. Medallions were set into the stone above the arches, each one with a gold name beneath—Bach and Haydn and more—that Lily was sure she ought to know and vowed on the spot to learn. Black iron gates guarded each arch, their gold spiked tops pointing up to the grandeur above, where the cast golden figures of the likes of Beethoven and Mozart observed the swarm of people below.

Lily had almost forgotten there *were* people around her passing the opera house as if they were used to being surrounded by such sheer beauty.

How can they not stop and look at it every time they go by? Lily thought. *I would never get used to it—never!*

"I'm going in," Art said. "You coming?"

Lily jumped. She had definitely forgotten Art was there. For a minute, it seemed like she was looking at a stranger. She could actually see light in his eyes—the old Art light.

"So are you coming in or not?" he said.

"We can actually go in?"

"Well, yeah. That's why it's got doors."

Lily could even shrug off Art's edgy voice. She was going inside the most beautiful building she had ever seen, and she held her breath as they crossed the street. It was like waking up on Christmas morning.

But as they passed beneath the arch protected by the face of Bach, she knew it was more than that. She was overwhelmed—mosaics on the floor, paintings on the ceiling, statues at every turn, candlelight shimmering down on it all.

Lily could barely climb the wide white-marble staircase that curved upward. It was hard to get past the two bronze statues of ladies holding bouquets of candles at the bottom. It was hard to pass *any* part of the place. She wanted to soak in each thing until she knew it by heart. But Art gave her a nudge, and she followed him up the steps.

"This is what they call the 'Grand Staircase,'" said a man behind them. He was reading a brochure to his wife. "It leads to the foyers and the different levels of the auditorium."

Lily slid her hand across the almost-purple marble of a small pillar at the turn of the staircase. *I didn't know stone could even be this color*, she thought, *or this smooth*.

She let her palm drift all the way up the marble railing as they climbed to the top. Then she noticed Art had stopped and was pointing to the ceiling.

"The four sections of the painted ceiling depict different allegories of music," Mr. Tourist Man read.

Lily didn't know about that. She just knew that the colors and the movement above her were almost dizzying. As soon as they had followed the flow of tourists into the circular hallway that surrounded the auditorium, she sank down onto a bench and waited for things to turn right side up again. While Art padded down the hall looking for an open door, Lily sat back and closed her eyes.

The bench was covered in velvet, rich and plush against her hands. Around her, voices murmured, the way they always did in Paris. It occurred to her then that Paris was a soft, humming place—so that the little things could be noticed, like the feel of the velvet-padded wall on the back of her head, and the whisper of a thought in her mind.

Gather the details. You will find me there.

Lily opened her eyes and looked around. Had somebody said that out loud to her? Or was that—God?

This isn't a church, Lily thought. *There isn't even anything Christian in here except maybe the angels. But I feel it. I feel God here.*

"Hey—psst!"

That wasn't God. It was Art, motioning to her from the curve of the hallway. Lily got up and hurried down to him. He was holding open a door padded with velvet that was tufted with brass studs. Lily let her fingers linger over it until she saw what marvels waited for her inside:

A round dome of a ceiling painted in reds and golds, with a dazzling chandelier hanging from it like a fountain of light.

A horseshoe-shaped auditorium filled with what Lily was sure were at least a thousand red-velvet seats.

A curtain draped across the stage, festooned with gold braid and pompoms.

Lily and Art stood in a small rounded balcony, looking down. Across the auditorium, another small group crowded into one identical to theirs.

Isn't it beautiful? Lily wanted to call to them.

A voice came back to her from the other balcony, and for a second, Lily thought she'd actually shouted and someone was shouting back.

But it wasn't a shout. It was a song, and two women were standing on their tourist balcony singing it, filling the air with sounds so pure, Lily once again had to catch her breath.

"What are they singing?" she whispered to Art.

"Opera."

"Are they some of the stars?"

Art shook his head. He had yet to take his eyes off the singers. "No," he whispered back. "I think they're just tourists. Italian, probably."

"How do you know?"

"Because only Italians can sing opera like that."

Lily looked up at Art in surprise. She wanted to ask

him how he knew *that*, but he had his eyes closed. His fingers were closed around the velvet railing, and she thought he was swaying—just a little bit.

I wonder if he's having an insulin reaction, Lily thought.

Whatever it was, it was smoothing out Art's face and taking away the steel-pole look of his backbone. For once, it looked like he was in a world that wasn't so dark. Lily tiptoed out and let him be in it.

Once on the other side of the door, she felt the stirrings of the butterflies in her stomach. Was she supposed to be alone here?

I'm supposed to be gathering details, she told herself. *I'm gonna do it while I have the chance.*

She remembered Mr. Tourist Man saying something about foyers, so Lily left the auditorium hallway and crossed the space where the Grand Staircase rose to her. She stopped for a moment to imagine the ladies of the old days swishing up those stairs in their elegant ball gowns. She decided that was why Charles What's-His-Face had made the staircase so wide.

Half-pretending to be wearing crinolines herself, Lily walked across the mirror-shiny marble floor, trying not to let her Nikes squeak, and passed between two of the columns that she was sure she, Tessa, and Joe together couldn't get their arms around. On the other side was the foyer, and when she saw it, Lily put both hands up to her mouth so she wouldn't cry out. *I can't take any more beauty! It's breaking my heart!* she thought.

Lily's chest did ache as she walked reverently down the columned aisle, hardly wanting to breathe or swallow in case this was a dream that could be snatched away by a heartbeat.

This must be where the audience comes during

intermission, Lily thought. *I wouldn't want to go back to the show!*

She didn't know where to look first. Above her, there was a vaulted ceiling covered with pictures made from tiny pieces of stone in sparkling colors on a gold background. From side to side, mirrors and windows captured the glow of the countless chandeliers. The rest of the ceiling was painted with figures delighting in the music they were making on lyres—those small harp-like instruments like the one on the statue outside. And at the tops of the columns, the heating grates and the doorknobs were all decorated with lyres.

Lily moved silently to the end where there was a round room, light and cool, welcoming her with yet another painted ceiling. Lily sank onto a velvet bench and looked up at it. She soon found herself smiling at the wood nymphs and fawns all fishing and hunting and splashing in different drinks.

I don't want to forget any of this, she thought. *I want to take it all home with me. Well, du-uh!*

She reached for her backpack in search of her camera, and then she remembered with a second "duh" that she'd given it to Mom to use. She thought about trying to describe it all in her notebook, but she didn't even move to look for it. *I don't know the words for it. I don't think there are any.*

But then on a second thought, Lily did dig out her notepad and a pencil. *If I can't take a picture of it, maybe I could draw it,* she thought.

She wasn't sure where that idea came from, but she began to sketch—a column top here, a tufted bench there. *An artist I'm not,* she thought. Curls, the boy in the garden who had drawn her, would be laughing his head off, she was sure. But still she let her pencil scratch softly across the notebook pages as she strolled, trying to capture just the details she wanted to gather up in her arms and carry back to Burlington to share with Reni and the Girlz—even if they had forgotten about her.

And she would need to take some details back to tell to Kimble over Jammy Dodgers, because Kimble might never, ever get to Paris. And she would have to gather even more details for Ingram, who would want to know how high the Grand Staircase was and how much the auditorium chandelier weighed. And Sister Benedict would want to know every detail about how she had seen and heard God in this incredible place.

The sketch Lily was making of the design in the marble floor suddenly blurred in front of her, and her chest was aching again.

I miss them, Lily thought. *I miss them all. I want to be here, but I want to be where they are too. It's so beautiful—and it's so sad.*

Enough alone-time. Lily closed her notebook and, still stuffing it and her pencil into her backpack, she left the foyer in search of Art. It was much quieter at the staircase now, and for one fear-pang moment, she wondered if he'd left her. Or was he in a corner having a reaction—and her without so much as a mint to give him? At this very moment, he could be lapsing into a coma in the men's room!

Even as Lily was making a vow never to leave the house without a snack for Art tucked in with her passport, she spotted him sitting on the top step. He was resting his chin on his folded hands. When Lily got to him, she saw moisture glistening in his eyes.

"You okay?" she whispered to him.

He closed his eyes. "Music," he said. "I need music."

Lily didn't have to ask questions. She just sank down onto the step beside him. They sat side by side for a long time.

It was late when they all piled into bed that night, and even later when Lily fell asleep. Every part of her was still tingling from the day and from the dinner for six at a place called Chez Clement, where Christophe translated the entire menu for them, gave their orders to the waiter, and sorted all the food out when it arrived. Lily had barely been able to eat for thinking about the opera house and the women singing and God whispering. Long after Tessa had finally stopped talking about how she used to think "Chris" was a jerk but now he rocked, Lily was still up thinking and writing and wondering.

I have never felt God like that anywhere, she thought. *I wonder—God—are you about to show me something? Am I about to find out who I really am on this earth? I think I know my mission right now,* she thought as she finally drifted off with Tessa's arm flung across her back. *I think it must be Christophe.*

The next morning, the sun was already high up on the window when she awoke. Mom was standing in the doorway with a mug in her hand.

"Is that hot chocolate?" Tessa said as she struggled to sit up.

"No," Mom said. "They call it coffee, but I think it's mud. I put half a pint of cream in it, but it still stirs like molasses."

"Why do you drink it?" Tessa said.

She had by now climbed out of bed and was on her tiptoes next to Mom, sniffing the air like she was double-checking to see if Mom was actually lying about the chocolate.

"I drink it because as long as I'm here in France, I want to do French things," Mom said.

"That's how I feel!" Lily said. "I want everything French!"

"Then you'll want to do French church. Get dressed, you two."

"Are we going to Notre Dame cathedral or someplace like that?" Lily said.

"Actually, we're going to Pastor Renee's church, and it starts in an hour. Let's get cracking."

Forty-five minutes later, the Robbins family, including Art, arrived at the mission.

"Where's the church?" Joe said.

"You're looking at it," Mom said. "I hear they really work a miracle on the gym every Sunday."

"How come he doesn't have a real church?" Tessa said.

"Hello! You cannot get enuff of me—no?"

Lily whirled around to find Christophe behind her.

"Well, don't you clean up swell?" Mom said.

Christophe's sandy hair was wet and combed up off his forehead, and he wore a T-shirt with no writing on it, tucked into his jeans.

Wow, Lily thought with a pang, *this must be his good outfit.* Joe wore better clothes to soccer practice.

"What are you all dressed up for?" Mom said.

"He's dressed up?" Tessa whispered to Lily.

"For the church," Christophe said. "I can sit by you?"

Lily blinked. "I thought you said church wasn't for you."

"But now you are here, Li-lee."

Lily was glad Joe and Tessa were already out of hearing range. Mom wasn't. She gave Christophe a long look, and Lily braced herself for—she didn't know what. The subject of some boy liking her and what she ought to do about it had never come up.

Why would it? Lily thought as she walked into the gym with Christophe behind her. *I'm not exactly a boy magnet.*

But at least she didn't feel like a boy repellent with dimpled Christophe sitting between her and Art during the service. He whispered translations and threw in a few of his own comments, as well—like, "You sing pretty, Li-lee."

Art leaned over at one point and said, "Lighten up, would ya, Christophe? I'm gonna need more insulin in a minute."

Christophe, of course, had no idea what that meant, and Lily didn't explain the whole thing about Art needing insulin when he had too much sugar. Art had made it perfectly clear that she wasn't supposed to talk about his disease to people. Besides, Pastor Renee started his sermon about then, and Christophe was whispering the translation non-stop in her ear.

The sermon was about Jesus forgiving the woman caught in adultery after everybody wanted to throw stones at her, and telling her to go and not sin anymore. Lily found herself nodding.

Okay, she thought. *That's what I'm supposed to do for Christophe. Everybody else—like that gendarme—just wants to punish him. But I'm gonna forgive him and teach him how not to sin anymore.*

She glanced over at him with his newly washed hair and almost-clean shirt. *Maybe I'm already being a good influence on him. He came to church, didn't he?*

She felt only a little bit disappointed that her reasoning was probably right, and it was not because he maybe had a crush on her. That couldn't have been what had brought him here this morning.

After the service, as everyone was folding up the chairs and rolling the altar back into a storage closet, Pastor Renee hurried over to the Robbins and began to make the rounds with cheek kisses. Joe and Art suddenly volunteered to carry chairs.

"Please to join Veronique and me for petite dejeuner," Pastor Renee said. "We have a special place."

"Do they have snails there?" Tessa said.

"Escargots?" the pastor said.

"No, snails."

"You have had snails?"

"No, I just want to watch somebody else eat them. It sounds gross."

"Gross is a good thing when you're ten," Mom said to Pastor Renee.

He threw back his head and laughed through the bushy black mustache. But then something seemed to catch his eye near the doorway. He sobered up and asked if they would excuse him for a moment.

Mom went off to retrieve Art and Joe, while Lily watched the pastor. He was joining Odette in the doorway.

Aw, man, Lily thought. *And it's been a perfect day so far.*

"You are sad, Li-lee?"

Christophe had evidently completed his quota of chairs because he was back beside her.

Lily pointed. "Your sister is here."

"It is not my day to watch her."

Lily spurted out a laugh. "Where did you hear that?"

"My man, Joe. He say that about Tessa. She is pain-in-the-neck—yes?"

"Don't hang out with him too much, Christophe," Lily said. "He'll teach you all kinds of bad stuff."

"Christophe!"

They both looked toward the doorway. Pastor Renee was waving him over. Christophe shook his head, but Lily gave him a gentle push.

"You better go. He looks kind of serious."

A cloud passed over Christophe's face, and he muttered something under his breath in French. His eyes had a hard, Art-like look as he turned to her.

"I see you tomorrow. More of my Paris—no?"

"Yes!" Lily said. *And I can't wait—to teach you about God, of course.*

Then she watched him join his sister and Pastor Renee and follow them outside. Then she dreamed about him in that same doorway tomorrow, his eyes full of new details.

She wished it were tomorrow already.

Nine

$\mathcal{L}$ ily was all prepared to talk to Christophe on Monday. Over lunch—*petite dejeuner*—on Sunday, Pastor Renee said so many things that she knew would help Christophe, she couldn't wait to get home and write them down in her journal so she wouldn't forget them.

It started when the pastor was teaching the Robbins kids about French table manners. Lily was watching everything Renee and Veronique did when they ate, and when they both set their pieces of bread on the table instead of on the edge of their plates, she did that too.

"Get your bread off the tablecloth, Lil," Mom muttered to her.

Veronique put her hand on Mom's. "I do not mean to eavesdrop," she said in her perfect English, "but here we always put the bread on the table. Bread is such a noble thing, it seems unjust to force it to share a plate with lowlier food."

She smiled and gave Mom's hand a squeeze. Both Joe and Tessa knocked their bread from plate to tabletop as if they were getting away with murder.

"What else do I need to know so my children won't embarrass me in public?" Mom said.

Veronique and Renee took turns telling them things like the gentleman always pours the wine—which children in France usually drink with their families from the time they are small—and the lady always pours the tea. Mom assured the kids that there would be no wine-drinking for them, but that she would be glad to man the teapot.

Renee and Veronique also explained why the waiter took away certain knives from the table when the kids didn't order red meat and replaced them with other, softer-edged knives. No unnecessary or inappropriate cutlery on the table, they said. And no loud talking in public places. The French as a rule were a quieter people than the Americans.

"You think?" Mom said. "France could be a wonderful influence on my children. I'm thinking of leaving them here permanently."

Veronique laughed her little tinkle of a laugh, but Pastor Renee grew serious, his eyebrows dipping low over his nose.

"You can be much more of an influence on France," he said. "You have faith that expresses itself in actions to help others."

"Yeah, but what's true faith?"

Every head at the table turned, because it was Art who had spoken. His eyes were narrowed like slashes of blue marker, but he was leaning forward on the table as though he really wanted to know. Still, Lily saw Mom's face tighten.

"Dude, we're gonna get another sermon," Joe muttered to Lily.

But Pastor Renee's answer was simple. "Faith is all about what happens between you and God," was all he said.

Art leaned back in his chair. "I don't think you could define what's going on between me and God right now as 'faith.'" Art gave a hard-edged laugh.

"You are talking to God?"

"Yelling at him is more like it."

"Then there is something happening between you. Do you also yell at your mother?"

Art gave a half grin. "I tried that. She didn't go for it."

"But you did not stop believing she was a real being when you were trying to yell at her."

Art shook his head. "But I thought faith was about thinking God's gonna make everything okay."

Pastor Renee's dark eyes grew wide. "Look around you, my friend. There are many faithful people in this world, but I do not see that it is all okay."

"Then why do we need God?"

"So that we do not become a part of that world which is not okay. So that we do not start believing in the world's power instead of God's power."

While the rest of the table tossed that one around, Lily sat silently making up her mind that helping France was going to start with helping Christophe. Now she *really* couldn't wait for tomorrow.

But although she hung around at the mission all day, from the time their home school started at 9:00 am until they left at 6:00 pm, there wasn't a sign of Christophe or his dimples. At noon Lily parked herself expectantly on the front steps, but by 2:00 pm she finally went inside so she wouldn't *look* like the forlorn little waif she felt like. By 4:00 pm she hid in Mom's office so Joe and Tessa would stop asking her where *her* "boyfriend" was so *they* could play soccer with him in the gym. By 5:00 pm, she was ready to hide her head in a bag.

I guess he's showing some other girl his Paris today, she thought.

When Christophe didn't show up the next day either, Lily took inventory of herself, trying to remember if she'd been pushy or bossy the last time she saw him. Those were the two main things people usually gave as reasons why she turned them off. But that couldn't be it, she decided, because he was the one who, on Sunday, had said he would be there to continue their tour of "Pa-ree."

Just to make sure, she got up the courage Wednesday night, when she and Art were both in the kitchen foraging for a snack, to ask him if he noticed her doing or saying anything that would drive a boy away.

He looked at her for so long that she wondered whether he was just trying to find something sarcastic enough to say. But when he did speak, he said, "You've really got a case for this guy, don't you?"

"I don't know what that feels like," she said. "It's too confusing."

Art just nodded soberly and said, "You've got a crush."

Lily glanced anxiously toward the pass-through where the TV was blaring out French on the other side.

"Just don't tell anybody else, okay?" she said. "Joe and Tessa are so immature."

"They're in elementary school, for Pete's sake. Of course they're immature."

"You know what I mean."

Art slowly peeled a banana. "Okay, look, I'll make a deal with you."

Lily winced. She'd made a deal with Christophe, and she'd never had a chance to hold him to it.

"You don't mention me having diabetes to anybody again, especially people who don't already know about it, and I won't tell anybody you've got a thing for Christophe."

"I can do that," Lily said. "Not that it matters. I bet

he's never coming back."

"Have you asked Pastor Renee about him?"

"No. Du-uh, I guess that would make sense."

"Ya think? He acts like he's his dad—and his sister's too. Now there's a scary chick."

Lily could have cared less about Odette, but she did have some hope about Christophe, now that Art had mentioned the pastor. She would ask him the next day.

But before she was out of bed in the morning, Mom announced that they weren't going to the mission.

"I told Renee I was taking the day off to take you kids on a little field trip."

"We're not going to the mission?" Tessa said. "What about the soccer game?"

"It's girls versus boys day!" Joe said.

"And we're *so* gonna walk all over them—"

"Yeah, in your dreams—"

"How soon will we be back, Mom?" Lily shouted over them.

"I'm so glad you're all excited about this outing," Mom said dryly. "The mission will live without us for a day. We're going to Clermont-Ferrand. That's where Pascal grew up. I'm told they have a great museum there."

"Who's Pascal?" Joe and Tessa said together.

"Is he that math guy?" Lily said.

Mom put her finger to her temple as if she were shooting herself. "I'm so glad I've spent the last six weeks doing science and math with you children. You've learned so much. Father of geometry, perhaps. Inventor of the first calculator. Major Christian who said we should all place our bets on God? Ring a bell?"

"Oh, him," Joe said.

Tessa just blinked. "I still don't know who you're

talking about."

"After today you will," Mom said. "Get dressed. We have a train to catch."

Lily told herself she was all too willing to get away from Paris for the day. *It's time to stop thinking about Christophe and get back to gathering details. Maybe I'm supposed to save France some other way.*

So she packed her satchel with her pilgrimage tools—and her passport—and, with her chin set in determination, took notes on the train about the villages they passed. She wrote about quirky houses, great stone barns clustered around churches, and fat white cows chewing in patchwork fields.

When the terrain changed from towns that took her mind back to the sixteenth century to factories that brought it screaming back to the twenty-first, she wrote those details down too. There were gray cheerless buildings, the rusted trains rotting away in abandoned train yards, the sooty-faced kids running along the tracks in bare feet.

I don't think they're doing that for the spiritual experience, Lily thought. *I bet none of them even owns a pair of shoes. I sure hope they have a mission here.*

Everything seemed to be in the shadow of the giant Michelin tire plant that puffed black smoke in the background, its smoke stacks rising up like church steeples. It provided all the jobs, Mom said, so Lily guessed it ran the town.

That evidently didn't make the people very happy, because the moment a traffic light turned green, the entire line of traffic began blowing its horns. Two angry young men with shaved heads glared at them out of a tattoo shop with a skull and crossbones on the window. The twisting, winding, alley-like streets were scarred by graffiti and marred by hole-in-the-wall stores that made Lily want to hide behind Art. When Joe stopped to gape into one called "The Evil One," whose wares all seemed to be dedicated to the devil, Mom grabbed his arm and pulled him along.

Lily was relieved when they finally turned a corner and found themselves in the center of town, which looked cheerier, compared to what they'd just seen. Just as in all the villages they'd seen on the way, there was a church in the middle of things.

"Why is it black?" Tessa said.

"Man, that's weird," Joe said.

Mom consulted her guidebook. "It's made from volcanic rock, guys. Says here the inside is almost nothing *but* gold gilt."

They checked that out, as well as the site of Pascal's birthplace, which turned out to be a piece of sidewalk with a circle containing his face placed in it.

"Impressive," Mom said. "What say we find the museum?"

There wasn't much enthusiasm for that, though there was more when they discovered that it was closed for renovation.

"That's it," Mom said. "Who's hungry?"

"Do they got a McDonald's here?" Tessa said.

"I don't know." Mom wiggled her eyebrows. "But I bet they have a pastry shop."

The *Salon de The*—The Tea Room, Art told Lily—had the best details of the day. Two glass cases that together were longer than the Robbins' apartment were filled with delicacies, and from what Lily could tell, each one was a work of art. Every pastry was perfectly golden and glazed to a gleam. Fruit was placed on tarts like jewels in a ring. Pastry was wrapped like fine paper around treasures of chocolate. Lily thought that if it was all as delicious to eat as it was to look at, she might not be able to stand it.

Mom told them to pick whatever they wanted, which took the better part of a half hour since that required not only looking at everything five times but asking what each thing was. Art could figure some of it out, and the lady behind the counter spoke a little English and made up for the rest. She smiled proudly over her baked goods and didn't even seem to mind that Tessa's voice rose about ten decibels with each new discovery.

Lily finally chose a *bicolore*, which meant "two colors." It was dark chocolate and white chocolate.

I'll probably get the biggest stomachache of my life, she thought. *But I'm eating every bite.*

But there was no pain involved. The pastry was so light it barely touched her mouth before it dissolved delightfully, and the chocolate layers lingered just long enough to leave her tongue begging for more. Yet she couldn't wolf it down the way she could a handful of Oreos. This was something to be savored, and she did with much oohing and aahing and stopping to think just how she was going to describe this in her journal.

Sacred details, she thought. *Definitely sacred.*

Since the day was "a bust, educationally speaking," as Mom put it, she let them spend the afternoon just exploring the city and stopping where they wanted to.

Tessa was fascinated by the street corner water fountains that merely spewed water from open pipes. It was all Mom could do to keep her from jumping into one of them for a swim.

Joe loved the old guard house they found on a side street. Mom read about it from the guidebook. If you were standing before the big door and looked up, the window above was set out so that there was an opening through which the person looking out could dump something on the head of the person at the door. Joe was disappointed that he couldn't try that on somebody.

For Art it seemed to be the park on the uppermost part of the city, where a man in a beret sat perfectly still while pigeons came to sit on his shoulders.

"I wanna do that!" Tessa said.

"I'm afraid you wouldn't get too much pigeon action, Tess," Mom said. "Do you see how quiet he's being?"

"Besides, they'd probably poop on your shoulder," Joe said.

They decided to hang out in the park for a while, and Joe pulled a small-sized soccer ball out of his backpack and challenged them all to a match. Only Tessa and Mom took him up on it. Lily and Art were sitting on a railing feeding the pigeons peanuts Lily found in the bottom of her bag, when two kids appeared out of nowhere.

They were both younger than Tessa, Lily guessed, and although they were bony and smudgy and wore third-hand-me-down-looking clothes, they had smiles as big and bright as—well, as Christophe's. Lily thought of him for the first time in hours, and it didn't make her happy.

"American?" said the boy. His teeth seemed very white against the dirty skin around his mouth.

"Yes!" Lily said. "Do you speak English?"

"We are very hungry," said the girl. "Do you have money, Americans?"

"Sorry," Art said.

"There must be a mission around here someplace," Lily said. "Maybe they could help you."

"We are very hungry," the girl said. "Do you have money, Americans?"

Lily frowned at Art. "Didn't she just say that?"

"Yeah. I think it's the only English she knows. Let's find out." He leaned toward the girl. "Are you aware that you are growing a second nose?"

"We are very hungry. Do you have money, Americans? Please?"

Her face was like a picture on one of those ads Lily was always seeing in magazines, asking you to sponsor a child in a Third World country. Her eyes alone, large and dark and tragic, were almost enough to send Lily scurrying over to Mom for an advance on the allowance money Dad had given her. But she didn't.

"I'm really sorry," Lily said. "But I just don't have anything for you."

She turned to pick up her bag, just in time to see a skinny arm yanking her billfold out of it.

"Hey!" Lily said, grabbing it back from the boy, who was already looking at her with wide-eyed innocence. "That's mine! Get your paws off of it!"

"So much for saving France," Art muttered. He stood up and waved his arm at the kid. "Go on—beat it. Get outta here before I call the cops."

The boy cocked his head. "We are *so* hungry—"

"*Gendarmes!*" Lily said.

The two kids beat it out of there without leaving so much as a cloud of dust.

"Pretty slick little operation," Art said. "One gets your sympathy while the other one's ripping you off. I guess that's the way street kids work."

"All street kids?" Lily said.

Art gave her a sideways look. "Maybe not all of them," he said.

It was well past midnight when they got back to the apartment, and Lily fell into bed with a promise to God to write in her talking-to-God journal first thing in the morning. For once, she was asleep before Tessa. But some time later, she found herself suddenly awake, and she wasn't sure what had disturbed her. Tessa was breathing evenly beside her, so it wasn't her having a bad dream. Lily decided it was just her imagination and sat up to fluff her pillow. There was a sound at the window, like something hitting the shutter.

Oh, man, Lily thought. *Is that one of the homeless people coming up to get us? Don't be a dope. It's probably a pigeon.*

She was about to flop back down when she heard it again, and this time there was a whisper too, as if it had been made purposely for someone on the second floor to hear. Creeping across the bed on all fours, Lily made her way to the window and put her head between the shutters just far enough to get a glimpse of the alley. What she saw made her stick her whole head out.

She saw Christophe looking back at her.

Ten

"What are you doing?"

Lily's whisper echoed down the alley. Christophe had to have heard it, but he didn't answer. Instead, he shinnied up a pipe attached to the side of the building until he was just a few feet below her. As she swung her legs out over the windowsill, she could hear him wheezing.

"What's wrong?" she said. "Are you sick?"

"It is my—oh—the—" He seemed to be groping for words the same way he was groping for breath. "I no know the word. Is fine." He waved it off with his hand. "I come to say good-bye."

"Good-bye? Maybe we could start with hello!"

"No. Good-bye for all the time. My sister don't can stay here. We are go away."

Lily had to hold onto the shutter to keep from tumbling out the window. Her mouth went dry. "Why? She's not the boss of you!"

A dimple crept into Christophe's chin. "Yes, she is boss. She make the money for me to eat the food. I stay here—I am send away."

"Why can't she make money here?"

"Pastor Renee say she cannot work—she must go to

school. There is job where we go. Real job. She will not have to working on the streets."

Lily felt her sharpest pang yet. The picture of the two little con artists in Clermont-Ferrand sprang to her head.

"My mother would no be happy if we start work on the streets," Christophe went on. "But a job—that she be happy."

"Where *is* your mom?" Lily said.

"Dead."

He said it so abruptly, Lily was afraid she'd made him mad, but he smiled up at her, a thin little smile that didn't reach his eyes.

"Good-bye, Li-lee. I like you."

"You can't go!" She put her hand over her mouth and glanced warily inside the window. Tessa hadn't moved an inch. Lily turned back to Christophe and spoke in a whisper. "Just don't go until morning. Promise me you won't."

"I no can wait—"

"Just meet me in the morning at 6:00 in the alley behind your market. Please, Christophe."

Finally, he smiled a Christophe smile. "0-kay," he said. "For you, Li-lee, I can wait."

You have to, Lily thought. She watched him slide back down the pole and disappear from the alley. *You just have to.*

She didn't sleep much the rest of the night as she formulated a speech to give to Mom. At 5:30 am, Lily crawled in on the foldout couch beside Mom and watched her face until she opened her eyes. She'd discovered a long time ago that was the best way to wake Mom up. She seemed to have a switch that flipped on when one of her kids was looking at her. That might have been because Art, at age two, had once slid a pencil up her nose while she was sleeping.

"What's the matter, Lil?" she said, voice still groggy. "Are you throwing up or something?"

"No, Mom—it's Christophe."

"Christophe is throwing up?"

"No-o. Listen."

In a series of whispers, Lily hissed out the story, ending with, "Can't we help so he doesn't have to move? He doesn't want to."

By then, Mom was sitting up and pulling her hair into a ponytail with the scrunchie she always left parked on her wrist while she was sleeping.

"I'm a little mystified about this job Odette supposedly has somewhere. Pastor Renee pays for their room and board so she can go to school instead of working."

"I don't know—but can't we do something?"

Mom swung her legs over the side of the couch. "Let me have a cup of coffee and I'll think about it. I'm sure there's something."

"There isn't time to think about it, Mom! If I don't meet him at 6:oo, I—we—will never see him again. Besides, I already have an idea."

"Why did I know that? Go for it. I'm listening—I can listen while I make coffee."

Lily trailed her into the kitchen. "Remember how you're always saying you wish you had more time to show us things here?"

"Uh-huh."

"Well—you could pay Christophe to take me around so I could see stuff you don't have time to show me."

Mom looked up from the coffee bean grinder, one eyebrow already up. "Is it the sights you're interested in or Christophe?"

"Both! I mean—I want him to stay here in Paris where

he at least has Pastor Renee—and us!"

"Are you being honest with yourself, Lil?"

Lily shrugged her shoulders up to her earlobes. "I like him. But it's not like he's my boyfriend or anything. I'm too young for that!"

"I don't think he thinks *he* is. He follows you around like a little puppy dog."

"I want to help him. I really do, Mom."

Mom didn't answer until she'd finished filling up the coffeepot with water. "I think your motives are pure, Lil, or we wouldn't even be having this conversation. But I'm not going to let you run around Paris without a chaperone, and I don't mean Joe and Tessa—although I think they could be relied on to tell all. And that isn't even my concern. I'm worried about your safety. You need somebody who is at least eighteen."

"You're talking about Art, aren't you?"

"Pretty much. Unless you want to call Dan and Betty."

"Hello!"

"Then I'd go wake up your brother."

"He'll throw something at me."

"I won't let him hurt you." Mom squinted at the clock. "It doesn't look like you have a whole lot of choice or a whole lot of time."

"Will you come with me?"

"I'm going to have a cup of coffee and get coherent, and then I'm going to call Pastor Renee and see if there isn't something more realistic we can do. Scream if you need me."

Then Mom turned back to the coffee-making, and Lily crept up the steps to the loft. Her heart had already sunk to the "anxiety zone" in her stomach.

To her surprise, Art wasn't buried under the covers

with a pillow over his head. He was sitting up in a chair that he'd pulled over to the round window, his feet up on the narrow windowsill. He was wearing his earphones, and he was jotting down words on a notepad. Both eyebrows went up when he saw Lily, and she braced herself for the hurling of the nearest projectile.

But Art just flipped closed the cover of the notepad and slid off the earphones as he punched a button on his portable CD player.

"What's wrong? Is Mom throwing up or something?"

"No! What is it with this family and throwing up—no, I came to ask you a question."

She took in a deep breath.

"No," he said.

"I didn't even ask it yet!"

"I can tell by the way you're getting yourself all psyched up that I'm gonna say no. Ask it."

She did.

He said no.

"Art, please!"

He picked up the notepad again. "Look, I'm really busy in the afternoons now."

"Doing what?"

"*No.*"

Then he looked at her with the same expression Mom used when that was the end of it. Feeling as if she'd just been poked and all the hope was leaking out of her, Lily turned back toward the steps. It was all she could do to hold back tears.

"You're way too nuts over this kid," Art said. "We're going back to Oxford in three weeks. You'll never see him again after that anyway."

Lily didn't turn around. "It isn't just that. I want to

help him find his details—"

"His *details*. That's a new one."

"That's where God is, and he needs God. He hardly knows what's right and what isn't—and he's sick too."

"He told you that?"

Lily heard the doubt in his voice, and she whirled around. "He didn't make it up or anything. I had to ask *him*. It was like he couldn't breathe—he was all wheezing when he climbed up the pole."

"Man, it was a scene from *Romeo and Juliet*—"

"Never mind," Lily said. Her voice went tight. "I'll just figure something else out."

Before he could see her really break down and cry, she hurried down the steps. Mom was in the shower, and Joe and Tessa were still asleep. Lily pulled out her suitcase and dug into the secret place until her fingers curled around the money from Dad. Pulling a sweatshirt on over her pajamas and stuffing the money into the pocket, she grabbed her shoes and stopped in the kitchen just long enough to scribble out a note to Mom: *I went to meet Christophe. I'll be back soon.* Silently, she let herself out the front door.

Paris was a different place so early in the morning. The streets were wet from overnight washing, and the shopkeepers were just pulling up their awnings and setting out their boxes of tomatoes and flats of artichokes. But Lily didn't care about this new set of details. All she could do was hurry by and pray that Christophe was going to keep his promise.

He was already there when she arrived, loitering around a pair of trash cans. His hair was sticking straight up on his head, and his eyes were baggy underneath. She couldn't tell if that was because he was sleepy or because he hadn't slept at all. It had never occurred to her until now to wonder where he did sleep. Mom had said Pastor Renee paid for his room, but what kind of place was it?

Suddenly the money in the pocket of her sweatshirt seemed like a pretty pitiful sum.

It has to be enough until I can get some more, Lily told herself firmly. *It just has to be. God—please let it be.*

"Li-lee? You are sad?"

"Of course I'm sad. I don't want you going off someplace!"

He managed a grin. "You cannot live without Christophe."

"It's you who can't live without me—"

"Oh yes?"

"Us! God!"

His skin puckered between his eyebrows.

"I know you don't get it," Lily said. "But you will if you'll just give me a chance. And it's not about the church, okay, because God just doesn't live in the church."

He was still looking at her like she was nuts.

"Okay, it's really hard to explain—especially back here—man, those trash cans stink."

Christophe plucked up a handful of her sleeve and pulled her away from them.

"I want understand, Li-lee," he said. "But there is no the time. Odette—"

"Forget Odette! You're going with her because she can make money, right?"

"Yes."

"I have money too. And there's more where this came from—I hope. There *will* be." She dug into the pocket and pulled out the Euros she'd folded so carefully. "Take this and buy what you need and then I'll—"

Christophe was already shaking his head. "This your money, Li-lee."

"So. You were going to take Odette's money."

"She is my sister."

"And I'm your friend. You have to take it, Christophe—or I *will* be sad."

"No sad, Li-lee."

"Then here." Lily took his hand, tucked the money into his palm, and folded his fingers down over it. "Just don't lose it."

Christophe only stood there, staring at his fist.

"Put it in your pocket before somebody sees it and you get mugged," Lily said.

She was about to take it from him and put it in his pocket herself when a voice at the end of the alley said sternly, "Stop!"

Lily and Christophe both whirled around to see Art standing there.

"Take your money back, Lil," he said. "Take it back right now."

Eleven

Art took the rest of the alley in two long-legged strides. The closer he got, the hotter Lily's face grew. By the time he was next to her, she was sure her head was going to explode.

"It's none of your business, Art! Just leave me alone!"

"Take your money back."

"No!"

"You are the boss of her?"

Art and Lily both looked at Christophe. He puffed out his suggestion of a chest and took a step to put himself between them.

"Oh, for Pete's sake," Art said. "Dude, just—"

"Art, *stop it!*" Lily stomped her foot hard on the alley's stones and shoved Christophe back to get to Art. "It's *my* money. Dad gave it to *me*—and if I want to use it to help Christophe, then I *will!*"

"Okay, so chill. I'm trying to tell you, you don't have to *give* him the money. He's gotta earn it." Art moved Lily aside by both shoulders and looked at Christophe. "You want a job?"

Christophe's eyes popped. "Me?"

"I'm sure not gonna hire Lily to show me around Paris

unless I wanna end up in Switzerland or someplace. My mother will pay you for every afternoon you take Lily *and* me for a tour, and she'll pay for all the Metro passes and bus tickets and all that. The only thing is, you have to take us to one required thing a day, and we have to do some kind of report on it or something." He put his hand inside his jacket and pulled out an envelope. "Here's some cash to hold you over 'til this afternoon. It's an advance on your salary. You know what that is?"

Although Christophe nodded, Lily wasn't really sure he was listening. He was staring at the envelope in Art's hand and the bills curled up in his own. It was as if he was trying to figure out how they'd gotten there. Then suddenly, he thrust Lily's money toward her.

"You will take this. I must earn my money."

He tilted his chin and straightened his skinny shoulders so that they looked twice their size. "I will rock!" he said.

Art shook his head. "You've been hanging out with Joe and Tessa too much. You've got to start learning your vocabulary from me, starting with who is the *boss* of whom. Madame Mama is your *boss*. You got that?"

"Yes." Christophe nodded until Lily started to imagine his head nodding right off and rolling down the alley. She wished Art's would.

First, he says no when I practically beg him. Then he shows up like this big hero—like having Christophe work as our tour guide was his idea.

If Christophe hadn't looked so proud right then, carefully pushing the envelope to the very bottom of his jeans pocket, Lily might have told Art to keep his stupid rescue to himself.

Just you remember one thing, Art Robbins, she wanted to say to him. *This is my mission on my pilgrimage. I'm not yelling at God like you are. I'm trying to listen to him.*

"We start today, noon sharp," Art was saying. "Be here or the deal's off."

Lily rolled her eyes. *What are we, the mafia now?*

But Christophe nodded soberly, and then grinned. "I got to find Odette. She will be happy."

"Whatever," Art said as Christophe danced his way out of the alley. "If that chick ever actually smiled, her face would crack like a puzzle."

Lily had to agree with him there. It softened her up enough to do what she decided was the God thing.

"Thanks," she said.

"Don't mention it. And look, our deal still stands. No going off about me being sick."

Lily blinked at him for a few seconds before she said, "Okay."

Art nodded toward the street. "We better get back before Mom sends out the gendarmes. She doesn't know you've been hangin' out in a dark alley at 6:30 in the morning."

"Hey," Lily said. "How did *you* know where I was meeting Christophe?"

"I heard you telling him."

Lily stopped and pulled him to a halt by his arm.

"You were spying on me?"

"No." Art took her hand off of his sleeve. "Chill. You think you're the only one picking up details in the middle of the night?"

He walked on, with Lily staring at his back the rest of the way home.

The next several days flew—*on the wings of happiness,* Lily wrote in her journal. She even made some sketches of herself and Christophe and Art all with feathered fins on their backs, winging their way across Paris.

I hope nobody ever actually looks at these, she thought as she drew. *It looks like some kindergartner did them.*

But it helped her remember every detail, and besides, she knew not even an artist could capture all that she was taking in by the basketful.

Each day they visited an official "sight" on the list Mom made for them. First they spent a few hours in the Musée d'Orsay—an art museum full of sculptures. Lily had to touch them to make sure they weren't alive.

Another afternoon, it was the Tuileries, a French formal garden that had been laid out for Louis the XIV—that was the Fourteenth, Lily figured out—where there seemed to be almost as many statues as there were trees. Although it was smack in the middle of the city, it seemed peaceful to Lily. The trees muffled the sound of the traffic so she could hear the birds singing and the children playing with rented toy sailboats in the pond.

Still another day, they walked along the Right Bank of the Seine River and viewed the Palais de Chaillot, a palace-like building that housed several museums. Although they went through a couple of them, Lily had more fun pretending it was still the country house of Catherine de Medici and that she, herself, was Catherine looking out from the piazza at the Eiffel Tower—even though it wasn't even there in the 1580s.

Art and Lily dutifully reported back to Mom on those things, and Lily looked them up in the books to make sure she hadn't missed any important facts to write down for Ingram.

But once the required must-see was done each day, Art would say, "Been there, done that," and then they would move on to "Christophe's Paris."

Every day, they took a trip on the Metro whether they

needed to or not. There were always musicians in the stations and sometimes on the trains themselves. There was a violinist who made his instrument sing to the workers on their way back to their jobs after lunch. Lily knew Reni would have stood listening to him for hours. There was also an old man who played on a harmonica, and a saxophone player who stopped Art in his tracks with his blues. Christophe and Lily waited patiently while Art hovered near him, eyes closed, swaying the way he'd done in the opera house.

I need music, Art had told her. Lily could see that he did.

After many trips under Paris on the Metro, Lily realized she had not once smelled anybody who appeared to be a stranger to deodorant.

"Mrs. Edwards is whacked," she said to Art.

"Totally," Art said. He didn't even ask why.

Another part of their daily routine was to have Perrier water and grenadine at a café, and they prided themselves on never going to the same one twice or ordering the same flavor back-to-back. Lily loved to watch the syrupy color swirl into the water. It reminded her of a ballet dancer.

The best part was when she found out she could say that to Christophe and Art, without one of them telling her she was a weirdo. Christophe gazed into his own glass and said, "My—what is word?—oh, carousel!"

Art twirled his glass in his hand. "A waltz. By Strauss."

Lily thought that must be one of the names on the opera house.

There were so many details in those and other places, Lily filled up the rest of her journal and had to start another one. She also used some of the Dad-money to buy a real sketchbook. As she looked over her drawings and her notes at the end of every day, it was almost impossible to decide what was *the* most important thing she'd learned in the last twenty-four hours.

Was it the fact that every door in Paris was different? She'd drawn a black one set into a stone alcove, a double door of glass surrounded by ivy so thick she could have gotten lost in it, a wooden one with brass fittings at the top of a set of steps flanked by luscious climbing roses, and an orange-painted one with a black ruffled canopy above it.

I don't know why I love the doors so much, she wrote in her journal. *Maybe it's because I feel so welcome here.*

Or was the most important thing how beautiful the people were? Some had dark chocolate-brown hair and deep dark eyes. Others were silky blonde with eyes like clear pools of blue. Everyone seemed to have creamy skin as rich as French coffee. Zooey, she thought, would be interested to know that there was barely a pimple in all of Paris.

It would have been enough to make Lily want to wear a bag over her head if Christophe hadn't been constantly telling her how *trés magnifique* she was. Although she laughed it off, she had to admit she did feel beautiful—especially when she was running in and out among the ash trees that lined the Seine in her bare feet, digging a little dirt out from beneath an old-fashioned light pole so romantic it made her want to cry, or lying in the soft grass at a *douceur de vivre* looking up at a cloudy sky that Christophe told her had just enough blue for a gendarme's pants and was therefore perfect.

The truth was that everything seemed important on those days, especially the things Christophe did for her and Art. The day before Art had to take an essay test for one of his correspondence courses, Christophe took them to the statue of the French philosopher Michel de Montaigne across from the famous university, the Sorbonne, in the Latin Quarter.

"There is custom with students," he told them, "to touch the boot before the exams for to—what is word—inspiration them."

"Why?" Lily said.

"He invent the essay."

"I don't know whether to rub his foot or punch him in the nose," Art said. Just to be on the safe side, he gave the old boy's toes a stroke.

Whenever Christophe spotted someone sitting in a window writing or looking as if she were daydreaming, he pointed it out to Lily so she too could dream. It was something he seemed to know she would want to do. One day, he escorted them to a crooked little bookstore called Shakespeare and Company and sat there beaming and dimpling while she climbed up ladders, squealing over books and smelling the oldness of some and the newness of others.

He also took them to the square where Victor Hugo's house was located. Lily liked the fact that this was the very *maison* where the author of *The Hunchback of Notre Dame* once lived, but she suspected Christophe had brought them there because there were musicians on every corner of the square. Art went from the guy playing classical music on the marimba to the mother and daughter on keyboard and cello to the twelve-piece string orchestra doing Mozart—who Lily definitely knew was up on the opera house wall—to the accordion player and the clarinet player who had just met that day and were jamming songs from the thirties and forties. Lily could see the dreams in Art's eyes as he watched and listened. It was enough to let her forgive him for horning in on her mission with Christophe.

At the end of every day, Lily realized that she hadn't really talked much about the things she'd intended to tell Christophe, like about God not wanting them to mess up the lives he'd given them by ripping people off and telling lies.

It's not that I forget, God, she wrote in her journal. *It's like you're just there so I don't have to point you out. I think Christophe sees you.*

Every night, she made a vow to put God into words for Christophe the next day, but every afternoon, Christophe seemed more and more like a God-kid to her. To say more than, "I think that's a God thing," when she noticed the fluttering dance of the ash leaves or tasted a fresh-off-the-tree olive for the very first time, seemed as ridiculous as saying to him, "Do you see Art here? Do you still see him? How about now?"

To her it was like all three of them were somehow enchanted and spiritual and full of God whether they were swinging their legs from a wall over the Seine or playing a game of pétanque in front of some random statue. *It is a God time,* she wrote. And for that, there was no picture she could draw.

Only one thing cast a shadow over that God time—Odette.

Twice when they returned to the mission at the end of the afternoon, Lily caught a glimpse of her working in the gym, checking out basketballs and leading little kids in circle games. Lily knew Mom had arranged that and was paying her, which she personally thought was a God thing. This way, their room and board were taken care of, and Odette had some of that spending money she said Pastor Renee never gave her.

But Odette evidently didn't think it was so godly. She wore a frown that looked too permanent—Lily thought it was probably engraved into her face—and she went about her work as if somebody were making her build the pyramids single-handedly.

When Lily mentioned that to Art, he gave a grunt, the first one she'd heard in about a week.

"You'd look tired too, if you walked around in stiletto heels all day." He peered hard at Lily. "Don't try to rescue her from herself, okay? We've got a much better shot with Christophe."

Lily bristled a little at the word "we." *I am the only one who even mentions God around Christophe,* she wanted to say to him.

And then Art surprised her. They were riding in the Metro one day and Lily was flipping through Mom's dog-eared guidebook. She came across a picture she'd looked at over and over. It was Notre Dame, with a round stained-glass window the caption said was a "rose window." She could almost feel God looking in and looking out of it.

"I still want to see this," she said.

"It's a church!" Christophe spat out like it was a dirty word.

Art sat back on his seat, his arm stretched out across the top of it so it almost touched Christophe's shoulder. "What's up with that? You've taken us everywhere we've wanted to go, but we mention the church and you get all bent out of shape. What's the deal?"

Christophe set his chin and looked out the window, even though there was nothing to see but a dark wall rushing by.

"Evil people there."

"Evil because—"

"Only evil. That is all I know."

"Come on, there's got to be some reason. What did

they do to you?"

"To my mother! They tell her *she* was evil—and she was not. She was the angel."

He turned again to the window, and this time Lily was sure it was to hide the tears she could hear threatening in his voice.

"I think that's enough, Art," Lily whispered.

But Art leaned forward and put his forearms on his knees. "I know you and Odette have had a hard time. I don't know if I could even have made it if I were you. But just because some church ran you out doesn't mean God's that way. Dude. I mean, he's here, which is probably why you two are still alive."

Lily could see Christophe watching Art's reflection in the window.

"He is not that way? Then how he is?"

"He's lookin' out for ya, man. Why do you think you've got this job, and Odette has the one at the mission?"

"Madame Mama," Christophe said. "She is boss."

"Yeah, and she listens to *her* boss—that's God. So does Lily," Art said, nodding in Lily's direction.

Christophe was still looking at the mirrored Art. "And you?"

"I do when I'm not being a jerk."

This time Christophe turned around to face him. "You are good. That is why God have the conversation with you. I—no good."

"You are not!" Lily said.

"That's not the way it works anyway," Art said. "None of us are good. That's why God sent Jesus to take our sins to the cross with him. You just have to believe that Christ died for you, and then talk to him on a regular basis. Then you *get* to be good because he helps you by telling you what to do."

Christophe suddenly looked three years old. His face got soft, and his brow puckered into tiny folds. "He will speak to me? Bad Christophe?" he said.

"No doubt," Art said.

But Christophe's face was still full of little-boy doubt as he looked at Lily.

"You think this, Li-lee?" he said.

"I *know* it," Lily said.

Slowly, the puckered face smoothed out. "Then I know also," he said.

The three of them rode the rest of the way in comfortable silence. *Talk about wings of happiness,* Lily thought. *I feel like I could fly right now.*

She was feeling so good about her sweet self, in fact, that when they got back to the mission and she saw Odette in the equipment room alone, Lily decided the only God thing to do was to go in there and at least try to be friendly. It didn't seem fair to just pour all the good stuff out on Christophe just because he was easy. Besides, she felt like God had her on a roll.

She dumped her backpack on the gym floor and headed for the room.

"Bonjour, Odette," she said as she stepped inside. The room smelled like old rubber and the kind of perfume Kimble always turned her nose up at because she said it was for tarts, whatever they were.

Odette turned from the cabinet she was locking. Her face went into a snarl.

"I just came to tell you that I have an extra pair of tennis shoes you could use if your feet hurt." Lily forced a giggle. "I can only wear one pair at a time. Matter of fact, if they fit you can have them."

Odette didn't seem to be too interested in that offer. She strutted right past Lily, heels scraping the floor. When Lily heard the door shut behind her, she sighed.

I tried, God, she thought. *Maybe the shoe thing was a bad idea.*

She turned around to go, and let out a gasp. Odette was still there, leaning against the closed door, her eyes in flames.

"I do not want anything from you, enfant," she said. "You have done enough."

"If you mean hiring Christophe, well, that's fun for us. I *just—*"

"You *just* betrayed me to Pastor Renee, that is what you did. I had a plan for going away and working a job that would pay for Christophe and me to live better than slaves. Now the man watches me like I am a criminal—worse than before—because the very special American girl has cast a spell on my brother. And for that, *enfant*"—Odette snapped her fingers—"you will pay."

And then payment began as she dug her fingernails into Lily's arm.

Twelve

*L*ily tried to pull away, but Odette's long, thin fingers were stronger than they looked, and her nails were sharp. The harder Lily pulled at her arm, the more it felt like a dartboard.

She couldn't think of anything to say to make Odette let go of her either. All that came to her was, *I never told Pastor Renee about you getting a job someplace else. I only told Mom! She had told him—*

But Lily stopped herself short. Tell on Mom? Mom wasn't the one who had started this whole thing.

Lily swallowed the lump that was swelling in her throat. *God, please help me say the right thing! Please—I'm listening! Give me a detail!*

"I don't know what you're talking about—me betraying you to Pastor Renee," she finally managed to say. "I'm just trying to help Christophe, that's all."

"Christophe is for *me* to help, not you. I am the one who has taken care of him since our mother died. I am the one who got us away from the people who drove my mother away and then when she was gone came to put us in a home for children. I am the one who found Pastor Renee—and I am the one who has decided he is no good for us anymore. I have always decided for Christophe, until you came along, Little Miss American Rich Girl."

"I'm not rich. I'm just—"

"You are just stupid. Not so special—just stupid."

Odette snatched Lily closer, so that she had to lower her face so their noses wouldn't touch. All she could see now was Odette's tattoo, a tiny round puzzle on her skin. All she could feel was Odette's hot breath on her cheek. All she could smell was the perfume and her own fear. It almost made her gag.

"Do not think for one *minute* that my brother cares for you, enfant. He only makes good use of you now, to throw you in the garbage bin later, where you belong."

Lily shook her head.

"You do not believe me?"

"No."

Odette let a hard laugh escape through her very-tight lips. "Then you *are* stupid, and you deserve whatever comes to you."

At last she let go of Lily's arm, but her eyes held on as she reached behind her, opened the door, and nodded for Lily to go. There was only a moment of relief for Lily. Once she was free of Odette's hands and eyes, Lily's heart pounded so hard she had to lean against the wall to get her breath. Her thoughts still panted in her head.

Is that true what she said about Christophe? Is he just using me to make money? Is he lying when he says I'm magnifique and all that stuff? Was he just pretending when he said he believed in God because I do?

Lily put her hand over her mouth to keep from throwing up. That couldn't be true. *Odette just hates me. She hates me so much she'll do anything to hurt me.*

But there was still one question she couldn't answer.

That question was, *Why?*

Lily didn't really want an answer to that. She just wanted to go home and sit on her windowsill until God whispered all of Odette's ugliness away.

Maybe Art will go home with me now, she thought, *before Mom and the kids get there. All I need is a little time.*

Art, she knew, was hanging out on the front steps the way he usually did when they got back to the mission. He always said he needed to regroup. He would probably be glad for an excuse to go back to the quiet apartment.

Lily stuffed her hands into her pockets so nobody would see them trembling and went into the gym in search of her backpack. If she could just grab it, tell Mom what they were doing, and get out of here without having to look at Odette again, she might be able to keep herself from tossing up her last Perrier and grenadine.

Keeping her eyes straight in front of her, Lily headed for the spot on the floor where she'd parked her backpack. Art's was there, but hers wasn't. She forgot about Odette and searched the area. There was no sign of it.

Panic she couldn't explain rose up in her chest, and she found herself gasping for air. Her heart slammed against the walls of her chest.

"Lil?" It was Mom. "Lil, what's wrong?"

"I can't find my backpack! I put it right there and now it's gone! It's gone!"

A strange quiet settled over the gym, and Lily realized she was screaming, but she couldn't stop. And the louder she screamed, the harder she breathed, until there were no breaths left to grab. Things started to go black.

"Whoa, girl," Mom said. Her voice went deadly calm. "Okay, everybody get back. Christophe—somebody—tell them to get back."

As if from very far away, Lily heard Christophe's voice barking out orders in French. She felt Mom pushing her to a sitting position and shoving her head between her knees.

"Relax, Lil," she said. "Just try to calm down."

"Here's her backpack," Lily heard Joe say. "It was way over there. What's the big deal about forgetting where you put your stuff?"

You don't understand! Lily wanted to scream at him. But there were no more screams left in her. She sagged into her knees.

"There you go," Mom said. "Atta girl. Take some deep breaths."

"Hey, Mom," Joe said. "There's another kid screamin' over there."

Lily could hear somebody squalling across the gym. In fact she was sure they could hear him all the way to Oxford. Her own head was clearing, and she lifted it as Mom put Joe in charge of her and squealed her sneakers across the gym to a now red-faced little boy who was pitching the fit to end all fits.

"Did he lose his backpack too, do you think?" Tessa said.

Lily felt herself go cold. It wasn't about a backpack, Lily was sure of that. Right next to the little boy was Odette, shrugging innocently at Mom one minute, and then when Mom was looking away, staring at Lily with pointy eyes. In one slick move, she snapped her fingers and then reached them out to stroke the boy's hair.

Keep my mouth shut? Lily wanted to shout at her. *No stinkin' way! I'm telling my mom the first chance I get!*

And then as if Odette were reading Lily's thoughts, she pointed at Tessa and then at Joe, who were racing toward the kitchen on Mom's orders to get the squaller some ice cream. With nails extended like a cat's claws, Odette drew her finger across her throat.

Do you get it? her eyes said to Lily.

Looks like I've got no choice, Lily's eyes said back. Slowly, she nodded at Odette.

Rocking back on her knees and hugging her arms around her own middle, Lily could only wonder what Odette had done to that poor little kid, just to draw Mom's attention away. One thing was for sure: She would do worse to Joe or Tessa if Lily told Mom anything. She had the wounds on her arm to prove it.

Her heart sank down to the "anxiety zone" and stayed there.

The next day was Saturday, and Mom announced over breakfast that they were going to take the fast train to Marseilles.

"Is that where the ocean is?" Joe said.

"The Mediterranean Sea," Mom said. "If all goes well, we'll stay overnight and spend some time at the beach tomorrow."

The cheer that went up was deafening. It was on the tip of Lily's tongue to ask if Christophe could go along, but Odette's warning was still strong in her ears and had been all night. Lily had been up for hours watching the alley cats crawl in and out of the trash cans in the alley and asking God to please tell her what to do. So far, he wasn't talking.

Although Lily had her notebook and pen on her lap on the train, she fell into an exhausted sleep almost before they left the Paris station. She woke up with Art shaking her shoulder.

"*What?*" she said. "I'm sleeping."

"The conductor's checking passports," Mom said from

across the aisle. "Get yours out and then you can go back to sleep."

"Yeah, definitely do that," Joe said. He was sitting in the seat facing her, flipping the pages of his passport. "You look pretty cranky."

"Stop making that noise with your passport!" Lily said. "It's too loud."

"Told you she was cranky," Joe said to Tessa.

"You want me to hit him for ya, Lily?" Tessa said.

"Yes," Lily said. "And do it hard."

"Right," Joe said. "And then I'll hit you so hard you'll spin around in your underwear without touching the elastic."

"*What?*" Mom said.

Joe grinned. "It's a French expression Chris taught me."

"Remind me to speak to Christophe when we get home. Lil, here's your backpack. Get your passport ready. This conductor looks even crabbier than you do."

"He must have been up half the night too," Art muttered to Lily.

"Why can't anybody just leave me alone?" Lily muttered back.

Then she ignored them all and unzipped the passport pocket of her backpack.

There was nothing in there. Last night's panic flooded her chest. Hands shaking, she pawed through the main compartment and the inside zipped pocket. No passport.

She turned the whole thing upside down on the seat and picked up her journal and her sketchbook. Waving their pages in the air produced nothing.

"What are you doing, Lil, your spring cleaning?" Mom said. She handed her passport and Tessa's to the conductor and leaned across the aisle. "I'll show yours to him.

Give it to me."

Lily knew her face was Cream-of-Wheat white as she looked up at her mother.

"It's not here, Mom," she said. "It's gone."

The next fifteen minutes seemed to pass in slow motion. Everyone in the family took a turn going through her backpack, and every one of them asked her what was with the plastic bag full of dirt. Once it was determined that she really didn't have her passport, the only questions were: "Why didn't you double-check before we left the apartment?" "Why did you ever take it out of your backpack in the first place?" "Why are you messing up our whole weekend?"

The conductor waved his arms and got red in the face as he hollered at Lily in foghorn French. Between Art and a college student sitting behind them, they were finally able to sort out that Lily would have to get off the train at the next stop, and that she wouldn't be able to get back on until the American Embassy gave her a temporary passport.

"You mean we're gonna leave her here?" Tessa said as the train screeched to a stop at the station.

"No," Mom said, in that low, calm voice that always struck fear even in Tessa. "We're all getting off. And it would behoove you to stay absolutely quiet until I get this whole mess straightened out."

Tessa didn't ask what *behoove* meant. The situation was that serious.

By then Lily was crying hard. The sobs cranked up two more notches when the gendarmes approached them before they had all their bags out on the platform. After an exchange of words with the conductor, amid much pointing, they informed Mom in broken English that they would escort the family to a taxi that would take them directly to the Embassy. They were not to leave there without a pass for Lily.

"If I don't get to go to the beach this weekend, you're dead meat," Joe said to her.

Mom turned around from the front seat and said, "Joe, don't say another word."

Nobody dared speak after that. Lily bit down on her hand so she wouldn't sob out loud.

It took five hours to get the necessary paperwork going. At one point, Mom sent Joe and Tessa out with Art to the McDonald's down the street so she could talk to Lily alone. The only good part of that as far as Lily was concerned was that Joe was finally smiling in anticipation of a Big Mac. He might not seek revenge on her for the rest of their lives after all.

"Lily, what on earth were you thinking?" Mom said when they were gone. "After all the preaching your dad has done, why would you leave your passport behind?"

"I didn't, Mom! I never even take it out of my backpack, ever!"

Trust me, she thought miserably. *After that thing with the gendarme and Christophe that day, I never go anywhere without it!*

"I hope you're wrong this time," Mom said. "Because if it takes this long just to get a temporary pass, heaven knows how much time it'll take to get a whole new passport."

"I'm sorry, Mom." Lily started to cry again. "I guess I'm not your sanity after all, am I?"

Mom let her lip twitch, and she put her arms around Lily. "Lil, my sanity left me the second day we were in France. I sure can't wait until your father gets here."

"Dad knows about this already?"

Lily's heart started an entirely new beat. Dad didn't

get mad that often, but when he did—

"No, he doesn't know about it," Mom said. "He called me last night and said he's coming for our last weekend here. He wanted to surprise you." She tightened her ponytail with a yank. "Don't tell the other kids, okay? At least let *them* get a kick out of it."

I guess I've given up my rights to a kick, Lily thought miserably. *Unless somebody wants to kick me in the backside for all this.*

By the time the temporary pass was done and Mom had "sworn her life away," as she put it, the last train had already left for Marseilles.

"We're going to have to make it another weekend," she said. "We're heading back to Paris."

Lily avoided the dagger eyes stabbing her from every direction and stared out the train window into the pitch blackness all the way back to the city. Joe and Tessa were still giving her the silent treatment when they all piled out of the cab at the apartment, but Lily hoped that Tessa would keep that up until she was asleep. The beating-up she was giving herself was bad enough. The first thing she was going to do when she got upstairs was tear the place apart looking for her passport.

But she was sidetracked by a note on their apartment door. Mom shooed them all off to their rooms while she read it. A few minutes later, she called Lily out into the living room where Art was already sitting on the edge of the couch. The pinch of anger was gone from her face. But her expression stirred up a new fear in Lily.

"What's wrong, Mom?" Lily whispered. "Is something wrong with Dad?"

"No," Mom said. "The note is from Pastor Renee. Christophe and Odette have disappeared."

Mom called Pastor Renee, and while they waited for him, everyone looked for Lily's passport, but it was nowhere to be found.

A knock on the door interrupted their search. It was Pastor Renee, who asked them if Christophe had mentioned leaving. Over and over, both Lily and Art assured him that Christophe seemed okay when they left him.

"We even had a kind of a breakthrough with him yesterday," Art said. "I thought we had him almost convinced that he oughta trust God."

"Then let us pray that he does that," Pastor Renee said. He tugged fiercely at the ends of his mustache. "That girl, that girl, that girl."

For a moment Lily thought maybe she ought to tell them about Odette's threats, but it just didn't seem as if it would do any good. She hadn't said anything about their leaving or where they would go if they did. Lily would even have felt relieved that she was gone—if she hadn't taken Christophe with her.

For days, he was all Lily could think of. Everything reminded her of him—every café, every patch of gendarme-blue sky, every detail. She stopped going anywhere because the whole Christophe-less world was painful. It was even too hard to write in her journal. Whenever she sat on the windowsill to try, she cried.

Why would he leave without telling me good-bye? she asked God over and over. *At least last time he did that much.*

There was only one answer to that, as far as she could figure, and she couldn't think about it for too long before she started to shake. What if Odette had done something that made him leave in a hurry? If she had, the chances were that it was something evil. Something very evil.

Lily had a nightmare about Christophe being turned

into a statue and hung up on the opera house. She couldn't eat without wondering if Odette had put a potion in his food. She broke into a sweat every time the phone rang, because she was sure it was Pastor Renee calling to say they'd found him passed out in an alley with the wild cats.

By the third day after Christophe and Odette had disappeared, Lily couldn't stand it any longer. While Mom was trying to drill long division into Tessa's head, Lily excused herself from their study room and went down to Pastor Renee's office.

He kissed her on both cheeks and started to pull out the pastry box, but Lily shook her head as she sat down. It seemed like so long ago that she'd come to this office for the first time. Back then her worst problem was finding a place to pour out a cup of espresso. She glanced at the wilted plant on the windowsill, and her heart ached for that time.

"You are troubled," the pastor said. "It is Christophe—no?"

"It is Christophe—*yes*," Lily said. "Did he leave a note for me or give you a message to tell me? Like maybe something you forgot in all the confusion?"

Pastor Renee's face-lines grew soft as he sadly shook his head.

"There is nothing—I am sorry. But do not take it to your heart so hard. Odette and Christophe have had a life very different from yours. They always must fight to survive, and it is difficult for them to take help from anyone." A trace of a smile passed through his eyes. "Odette is stubborn. I have fought with her many times."

"Oh," Lily said. "I think I knew that."

Pastor Renee sighed so deeply that Lily thought he would deflate before her eyes.

"I thought perhaps Christophe had a chance, especially

when you and your family came. But he is loyal to his sister." Pastor Renee came over to sit next to Lily, folding his hands in his lap in that careful way he had. "When Christophe and Odette were very young—Christophe was only a small baby—their father left them and their mother, Marie Claire, and when she went to the church for help, they turned her away."

"Why?"

He shook his head sadly. "Who knows? Some people, even in the church, have no compassion."

"What happened?" Lily asked.

"Their mother tried to care for them. She took a job, but—it was not so good. I met her when I first began as a minister to the struggling people of Paris. I tried to help her, but soon after that, she died."

"What happened to her?" Lily said. She could hardly talk for the lump that was forming in her throat for Christophe.

"No one knows for sure. She was found—" Pastor Renee waved his hand as if he could hardly speak either. "Odette was then twelve years old. They stayed in foster homes for many years, and then she ran away with Christophe for a time. When she found me again, she and the boy were nearly starving. I have tried to be like a father, tried to keep them together, but it is very difficult. Odette is proud—she feels she is like a mother to Christophe. The only reason the authorities do not place him in a children's home is because she is old enough to be his guardian. And he—well—he is devoted to her. Now she has bigger and bigger ideas—dangerous ideas—and Christophe cannot turn his back. Sometimes our greatest strength is also our greatest weakness—no?"

"I don't want her being his weakness! I want him to

forget about her! But he's forgetting about me—us."

"No, no. Christophe will never forget about you or anything he has learned from you and your family. You have made a difference in his life."

"I don't think so," Lily said. "But thanks for saying that."

Pastor Renee put his hand on her shoulder. "Christophe told me about the details you look for. No detail of God's work is ever wasted. You will see."

Pastor Renee prayed with her then and sent her off with the whole box of pastries. That did a lot to return her to Joe and Tessa's good graces, but it didn't make Lily feel better. When even her new passport arriving in the mail didn't cheer her up, Mom came into her room while the other kids were watching *The Princess Bride* with subtitles and closed the door.

"Lil," she said, "I'm really concerned about how hard you're taking this thing with Christophe. I don't think it's because you had a crush on him. Am I wrong about that?"

Lily shook her head. She was afraid to talk, afraid her heart would rip right open.

"Then what is it, Hon? You can tell me anything. You won't be in trouble, I promise you that."

Lily measured out her words. "It's my fault."

"What's your fault?"

"It's my fault that they ran away. Odette hates me and that's why she took him!"

"Lil—Hon—I think you're letting your imagination run a little wild."

"No, Mom! She attacked me! In the equipment room at the mission—only I was afraid to tell you because she threatened to hurt Joe and Tessa. I didn't talk to him about God enough, and I've messed up my whole mission. I can't do my pilgrimage, and God's disappointed in me because I can't do the one thing I think he really *does* want me to do after all these years of trying stuff. Now he isn't even talking to me, and I'm so ashamed!" Then she buried her face in her pillow and cried and cried and cried.

"Lily, Lily, my angel from heaven," Mom said when there were no more tears to cry. Her voice sounded thick. "I can't even sift through all that right now. But I do know this. Sit up and look at me."

Lily did, although she could barely see Mom through her tear-puffed eyes.

"You are Lily Robbins—which means you will always be on a journey to find God's place for you in this world. You are Lily Robbins—which means that place will seldom stay the same for long. You've taught me that yourself." She brushed wet hair away from Lily's cheek. "Please don't waste another moment of your time here fretting over what you haven't done. Just ask God what he wants you to do now in *your* life, and leave Christophe and Odette to him. Will you promise me you'll do that?"

Lily nodded, because there were tears in Mom's eyes. And that was something a Robbins kid almost never saw.

When Mom left the room, after offering to let Tessa sleep on the foldout couch with her that night so Lily could be by herself, Lily went to her windowsill and waited for the household to fall asleep. Only when it was quiet could she close her eyes and say, *Please God—what next?*

But it wasn't silent, not yet. Below in the alley, litter crunched underfoot. Maybe it was alley cats again or some hungry, homeless person.

"Go away, kitties!" Lily hissed to them.

"Is no kitties, Li-lee," said a voice. "Is me."

Lily only remained frozen in the windowsill for a

moment before she swung herself out onto the pole and slid down. A surprised Christophe waited for her at the bottom. She was so glad to see him, that she hugged him quickly, before pushing him away and shaking him in frustration.

"What were you *thinking?*" she whispered to him hoarsely. "Why didn't you leave word for me if you had to leave so fast with Odette? Why did you have to go with her at *all*, Christophe?" She put her fingers to her temples and closed her eyes. "Never mind all that. I'm just glad you guys are back. You don't have to explain anything."

"*We* are not back," Christophe said. His voice was jagged. "Only *me*."

"Odette left you?" Lily said. She squinted through the dark into his eyes. They were so frightened that they made Lily's hands begin to sweat. "What's going on?" she said.

By now Christophe could barely speak. It was as if the fear were holding its fingers around his throat.

"Odette—she has gone to a place I cannot go without the passport."

"How can *she* go there then? She doesn't have a passport, does she?"

Christophe pulled his gaze from hers and looked at the ground.

"Christophe, *what?*" Lily said. "Talk to me!"

"She does have passport now, Li-lee," he said. "She has yours."

Thirteen

Odette has my passport?" Lily said. "How—"

But she didn't really have to ask. Her mind rewound like a tape to the day at the mission when she hadn't been able to find her backpack. It was the same day Odette had trapped her in the supply room. And it was the same day she had threatened to hurt Joe or Tessa if Lily breathed a word to Mom. She'd been so afraid that she had cried herself out of control over a stupid backpack that was missing for five minutes.

But there were no tears now, no pounding chest, and no fear that Joe and Tessa were going to be kidnapped by a girl with killer high heels. Lily took a step closer to Christophe. He was clutching his arms around a body that no longer looked like it could stand up to an angry gendarme who had just caught him stealing flowers.

"Come on, Christophe," Lily said. "We're gonna go tell my mom."

Christophe's face came up, and his eyes began to beg before his mouth did.

"Please, Li-lee," he said. "Please, no. They will put me in the home!"

Lily curled her fingers around his sleeve, just the way

he'd done around hers so many times.

"We have to tell her," she said. "She'll know what to do. God's her boss—remember we told you that?"

"No, Li-lee. I only come to say good-bye. To—what is word—warn you. The gendarmes will take you to the jail if you no have the passport."

"I already did the thing with the gendarmes! We had to go to the Embassy and everything. Christophe, it's not like taking something from that nice lady at the grocery. We're *kids!* We need Mom—now come on."

Christophe's shoulders, always so squared to meet his Paris full of shady Metro stations and motorcycle men, curved like the top of a question mark.

"I must give up, then. My mother say we never give up."

Lily shook her head as she tugged at his sleeve. "It doesn't feel like giving up, Christophe. It just feels like a God thing. I *know* that when it happens—I just do—and this is it."

Christophe searched her face with eyes so frightened that it was as if he were looking for an escape route there. "You are sure about this, Li-lee?"

"That's why I'm always gathering details. That's how I *know*. Now come on—"

"Hey—alley cats."

Lily snapped her head back. Above them, Art was hissing to them, his curly head silhouetted in Lily's window. He looked like an angel cut loose from the opera house—a *rescuing* angel, as far as Lily was concerned.

"Help us up, Art!" Lily whispered hoarsely. "There's a pole here—"

"How 'bout I just let you in the front door?"

"Oh yeah, huh?" Lily said. For once, she was glad to hear Art grunt.

When they reached the living room, Mom was already sticking her ponytail into the scrunchie and climbing out of the sofa bed. Her eyes, baggy with sleep, seemed to be trying to absorb the fact that Christophe was there, now clinging to Lily's sleeve even as she hung onto his.

"Madame Mama—she will hate me now," he kept whispering to Lily.

"Mom doesn't hate anybody," Lily said.

"Hate you?" Mom stood up and pulled Christophe into her by the back of the neck so she could hug him. "I've never *been* so glad to see somebody. Where is Odette?"

Christophe shook himself away from Mom and backed toward the door, bumping gently into Art.

"She's gone," Lily said. "With my passport. Well, my *old* passport."

Art gave a long, low whistle.

"Okay, I think we'd all better sit down for this one. Lil, hand me my bathrobe, would you? Christophe's shivering like a wet dog."

Lily and Mom got Christophe wrapped in Mom's robe and propped on the sofa bed before Mom would let anybody ask any questions. Lily was glad about that. It gave Christophe a chance to go from looking like a whipped puppy to just a kid with some explaining to do to his mom. With a lamp on in the corner of the room, a glass of milk tucked into Christophe's hand, and the faint smell of Mom's nighttime face cream in the air, things didn't seem as bad as they had down in the alley with the trash cans.

Mom perched on the arm of the sofa, leaned her arms on her knees, and said to Christophe, "Let's start at the beginning, Pal. Where did Odette get Lily's passport?"

Christophe only stared down into the milk.

"I know, Mom," Lily said.

"No, Li-lee. You do not know."

"Odette took it out of my backpack that day at the mission when we came back from—"

"No."

"Yes, she did! It was missing for about ten minutes."

Mom put her hand up to Lily. "What happened, Christophe?" she said.

He didn't answer.

"Look, son, there is nothing you can tell us that is going to make us hate you or stop caring about you or whatever it is you're afraid of. We just want to help. That's all."

"Dish, dude," Art said.

Christophe looked as if he would rather dive into the glass of milk and drown.

"Odette did no take the passport," he said. "I take it."

The room was silent. Lily felt herself going cold.

"No way," Art said finally.

"Yes. Way. Odette tell me she will go—make the money—come back for me so we don't can continue the living as we do. She say we not *steal*—we—what is word?"

Art gave a soft grunt. "Borrow?" he said.

"Yes. She will bring back—two weeks. I think it is okay. Only now I know. You have teach me that it is no okay. Before, when she tooked the camera, I think it is okay. I try to tell her no more—" He looked at Lily with misery in his eyes. "But she is my sister, Li-lee."

"She's a piece of work is what she is," Art said.

Mom put her hand up again. "So where did she go, Christophe? Did she tell you?"

Christophe shook his head. "I want to follow her—but I have no passport. And she is clever—Odette."

Mom nodded. "We definitely can't underestimate that. She couldn't have gone too far without money. I hadn't paid her for the week yet—"

"She have money. She take the money *I* earn from the tours." He cocked an eyebrow at Mom. "*This* make me angry."

"No doubt," Art said. "I'd have followed her to China if she'd ripped *me* off."

"No without the passport."

"She won't get far," Mom said. "The first thing any official is going to see when he looks at the picture on the passport is Lily's red hair. She might be able to pass for Lil otherwise, but that's a pretty obvious feature—"

Christophe was shaking his head. "Odette has the red hair now. She—what is word?"

"She dyed her hair?" Art said. "Dude—this chick is serious."

"A little too serious." Mom unfolded herself from the arm of the sofa and padded toward the kitchen. "I'm going to call Renee. Art, you have a T-shirt Christophe can sleep in, don't you?"

Art nodded and headed for the loft. Lily was left alone with Christophe, but she couldn't look at him. She could only close her eyes and listen to what was going on in her mind. The memory-tape had already rewound to that day when Odette threatened her in the supply room.

It wasn't just any stupid day. It was the day the three of us were talking on the Metro train. We were telling Christophe about God. Art told him God would speak to him. And then I told him I thought God would speak to him too. That I knew it.

Everything began to sink in. Even her eyelids felt heavy as she closed them. "*Then I know also,*" Christophe had said. And Lily had felt like she had wings of happiness—wings that flew her straight to Odette to try to make friends.

When she began to imagine Christophe taking her passport out of her backpack, Lily opened her eyes. Christophe was watching her, but when she looked at him, he turned his face away. She could see him swallowing.

"You planned it even before that day, didn't you?" she said. "You had it all planned out that day you were talking about your mom on the Metro and we talked to you about God. You knew right *then* when you were all smiling at me and telling me you believed too. You knew right then that you were going to steal from me!"

"Then is true."

Lily chewed at her lip and blinked at him. "What's true?"

"My sister tell me, 'Do not to trust the rich Americans. They will never forgive you.'"

Then he watched her, as if some little lip curl or eyebrow twitch would give him his answer. Lily knew what he was looking for. He was looking for details.

The only ones she could give him were the ones that came to her. She pushed her hair behind her ears, tilted her chin up at him, and shook her head.

"Odette is wrong," she said. "I forgive you. It's the God thing to do."

"All right, my friends," Mom said. She came in briskly from the tiny hallway with a pillow and a blanket in her arms. "Pastor Renee is coming over first thing in the morning. Christophe, you're staying with us tonight. You can bunk upstairs with Art." She plopped the pillow and blanket into his outstretched arms. He took them without a word.

"Off to bed, Lil," Mom said. "In case nobody's noticed, it's still the middle of the night. Sleep in tomorrow." She squeezed Lily's shoulder. "Everything's going to be taken care of."

But Lily wasn't sure she could sleep at all. She noticed that Christophe went dutifully upstairs to the loft without giving her another glance.

I don't know whether he believes me or not, God, she wrote in her journal. *I think I've messed up this part of the pilgrimage. But please don't let him be taken away to jail or something. Please, God. Please save him. I guess I can't.*

She crawled in beside Tessa, who seemed to sleep through everything. Lily was sure the Eiffel Tower could fall on their apartment building and Tessa would still be snoozing.

I wish I felt that peaceful, Lily thought. *Mom says everything's gonna be all right, but I don't see how. Odette's gone. I know she'll never come back with money for Christophe. He'll have to go off to an orphanage or something. I'll never see him again. Not ever.*

It was a sharp, pointed thought, and she couldn't go to sleep with it. There had to be another thought—an idea—some way to make Christophe believe.

He doesn't believe me. Not like he does Odette.

Odette. Lily had to admit it as she fell into a fitful sleep; Odette was the one detail Christophe needed.

When Lily woke up, the sun was slanting through the window from above the building across the alley. It had to be at least noon.

Lily looked around frantically. Tessa was gone. The sofa bed in the living room was neatly made up, and there was no sign of Joe or Mom either. The only sound in the apartment was music curling down in wisps from the loft. Lily took the steps up two at a time. *What if they've already* taken Christophe away? What if I've missed my chance to say good-bye? she wondered.

But as she burst into the loft, Christophe was sleeping in Art's bed, the covers pulled up so that all she could see were a few freckles on a sleep-breathing nose and some sand-colored hair spiked up like that of a two-year-old.

Art was sitting on a chair with his back to Lily, his headphones obviously blocking out everything. It took Lily a few blinks to realize that he was singing. He held a notepad in his hand—the one Lily had seen him writing in before. It looked to her as if he were singing the words he had put there.

He stopped, pulled the earphones down around his neck, and scratched something out on the pad.

"Art?" Lily whispered.

He looked over his shoulder.

"Where is everybody?" she said.

He pointed to Christophe and then to the steps.

"They went to the mission," Art said when they were both in the kitchen. "I'm supposed to make sure you two eat when you get up. I make a killer peanut butter sandwich. Only we don't have any peanut butter."

There was something so kind in his voice that Lily burst into tears. When Art put his arm around her and held it there, she cried harder.

"There's gotta be something we can do," she said through her tears. "I wanted to save him."

"You read too many chick books," Art said. "It's not like they're gonna stick him in some dungeon orphanage. They've got government agencies—"

"I don't mean that! I was trying to help him believe in God!"

Art's arm got tighter around her shoulders. "Okay, I'm

blowin' it here. Look, Lil." He let go of her and turned her to face him. His hands went into his pockets as he tilted his head at her. "I understand this whole thing about not being able to change the situation. I've got diabetes in my face 24/7. But I've finally figured out something. You can't always change what's happening, but you can change *yourself.* I'm doin' it—you're doin' it. You're like this whole other person than you were back home."

"Sister Benedict said that," Lily said. She wiped her nose with the back of her hand and kept crying. "She said things are always changing when you're—when you're on a—a—pilgrimage."

She looked closely at Art through her blur of tears, but he wasn't rolling his eyes. He was nodding, as if he got it.

"I've been looking—for the—the God details," Lily cried, "so I'll—stay on the journey—you know?"

"Ya think? I've been followin' you all over Paris collecting details. It's like watching you put together a puzzle."

"But it didn't help! I can't save Christophe! I don't think he believes, even after everything. That's the journey I thought I was on."

"Okay, look." To Lily's amazement, Art put his hands on her shoulders. He bent his head down so she had to look at him. "We've all got our own journey. Who am I to tell you what yours is? But I'm watching you every day—like I had a choice, right?—and what I'm seeing is that the kid who always had to go ballistic over everything is disappearing."

Art looked at the ceiling as if he might find his next words there. "You used to be like 'I gotta find my thing so I can fix everything and if I just throw myself into it hard enough I can do it.' It used to drive me nuts. It used to drive everybody nuts." He shook his head. "Now I'm seeing this real person on a journey looking for God in every little flake on a croissant, for Pete's sake, and it's not driving me nuts. It's making me look for my own details."

He tightened his fingers on her shoulders. "Tell anybody about this back in Jersey and I'll cut your heart out—but it's like you've been teaching me how to find out who I am now. Everything is different because I have diabetes. But the difference in me is good because it's forced me to find out who I am and who God is. I'm real, and so are you."

Lily had stopped crying, and she found herself searching Art's face looking for things to savor, because this was a God moment. In a second, her big brother would let go of her and make her a rubbery grilled-cheese sandwich and probably tell her to chill. But right now, he was looking at her like they were grown-ups who knew about pilgrimages and sacred details and things a lot of other people didn't understand. People like Christophe.

She felt herself sag and pointed upstairs. "How does this help him?"

Art let his arms drop and picked up a paper bag on the counter. "This is from yesterday," he said as he peered inside. "It's probably like a big crouton by now, but I could smear some butter on it for ya. I think we keep looking for details."

Lily smeared at her nose again. "In the bread?"

"No. In Christophe. That's how we help him find God and his own self. Details."

Lily grabbed a napkin and blew her nose on it.

"Nice," Art said.

Lily hiked herself up onto the counter and took the hard chunk of bread Art handed her.

"Maybe we oughta dip it in something," he said, surveying the contents of the refrigerator. "How about a Diet

Coke?"

Lily nodded absently. "The only details I can think of about Christophe are the dimples on his chin."

"He's got dimples on his chin?"

"And the way he pops a whole bunch of cherries into his mouth at once and makes his cheeks bulge out."

"Keep going."

"And the way his eyes get all sad when he talks about his mother. And they get all mad when anybody even mentions the church."

"We know why that is," Art said. "Not much we can do about that. Besides—the church taught him there was a God in the first place, and he *used* to believe."

"Do you think that counts?" Lily said.

"To God, you mean? Yeah. But whether Christophe trusts him is what we're really going for here." Art chewed thoughtfully and looked at his bread. "This isn't half bad dipped in Coke. Don't tell Pastor Renee—he'd probably pass out." He stopped and looked toward the bottom of the steps. "Speaking of passing out—hey, dude, you gotta be hungry."

Lily turned around to see Christophe leaning against the steps, his face waxy pale.

"I am not hungry," he said. "But I have think of the detail."

"What detail, man?" Art said.

Lily slowly slid off the counter. She was hearing a sound coming from Christophe that she'd heard before. A wheezing sound. That was one detail *she* hadn't thought of.

"I know I'm not supposed to talk about this," she said carefully, "but are you sick again, Christophe?"

Christophe shook his head, but his wheezy breathing grew louder.

"What's going on, dude?" Art said. "It sounds like you

have asthma or something."

"Do you, Christophe?" Lily said. "Is that what's wrong with you?"

Christophe was shaking his head wildly. "No—no—listen to me!"

Lily put her hands up to her mouth. Christophe looked as if he were close to tears.

"I have think of the detail," Christophe said. "I know where my sister—she go."

Lily forced herself not to spew out a hundred questions. Beside her, Art was nodding at Christophe.

"I think about the art—here—on my sister." Christophe pointed to his shoulder.

"Her tattoo?" Lily said.

"Yes. That is where she is. I can find her."

"I *so* don't get this," Art said.

But Christophe was already headed for the front door.

"Where are you going?" Lily said.

"Hey, Dude! You can't just go running after her—you don't have a passport!"

"I do not need the passport," Christophe said from the door. "Odette—she never leave Pa-ree."

Fourteen

Art and Lily both yelled all the way down the alley to the street, past the market, and past the café. But none of their pleas stopped Christophe. He didn't stop running—and neither did they—until they were on the Metro platform with the train barreling toward them.

Then he bent over at the waist, his hands on his knees. He was breathing so hard the wheezing could be heard over the squeal of the train as it stopped in front of them. Christophe climbed on and slumped into a seat with Art and Lily right behind him.

Lily fell onto the seat next to him. Art sat on the edge of the seat across from them, so that his nose nearly touched the top of Christophe's head. The boy was still gasping for air.

"First of all, you better slow down, dude," Art said, "or you're gonna end up in the hospital."

"No—I will find Odette."

"You can't, man. She's leaving the country—remember, the passport?"

"That was—what is word? Odette—she is clever—she say, 'Christophe—I need passport because—'"

He stopped and wheezed until Lily was sure his lungs

had deflated like balloons.

"Chill, man," Art said. "You aren't making any sense anyway."

But Lily suddenly knew that he was.

"Christophe!" she said. "Do you mean that Odette did all that with getting you to steal the passport and dying her hair to make you *think* she was leaving France?"

Christophe nodded. He was coughing so hard now that he could hardly talk at all.

"Okay, I'll buy that," Art said. He looked at Lily. "But where is she?"

"Something to do with the tattoo," Lily said.

"Great. It was so small that I could never see it." Art put his hands up. "Not that I was ever looking that close." He twisted his head so he *could* look up close at Christophe. "How you doin', man?"

Christophe sat up, but his breaths were still coming hard. They made Lily's chest hurt, and it was already aching with her heart trying to hammer its way out.

Christophe held up his finger and thumb as if he were trying to make a tiny circle.

"The tattoo?" Lily said.

Christophe nodded.

"It's a circle?" Art said.

"Yeah," Lily said. She closed her eyes and tried to remember. "It had little tiny designs in it, only I didn't really get *that* good of a look at it."

"No-tra," Christophe said. His voice was hoarse, as if it were being squeezed from his throat.

"No what?" Art said.

Lily gave a gasp. "Notre Dame, Art! He's talking about the cathedral! The tattoo's like the rose window!"

Art looked blankly at Christophe. "Odette went to Notre

Dame? No way, dude—the church is the *last* place she's gonna go!"

The high squeal of metal on metal was bringing the train to a stop, and Christophe stood up. He was breathing so loudly that he was attracting stares. When the doors opened, he pushed past two of the gaping passengers and jumped onto the platform. From over their shoulders, Lily saw him tumble to the concrete.

By the time Art got to him, Christophe was already struggling to get up. Lily joined them and grabbed the arm Art didn't have. Christophe didn't resist them. Tears were spilling out onto his cheeks.

"Please, Li-lee," he said in a voice she could hardly hear. "My sister cannot go to this place. These people are evil. She go to get money. She promise me she will not—but I know."

And then all Christophe could seem to do was shake his head and cry and say, "Please, Li-lee."

"Art, we have to do something!" Lily said. Panic was rising up in her throat.

"Okay, look," Art said to Christophe. His voice went low, the way Mom's did when she was deadly serious. "We have to calm down and get this all straight or you're gonna go down right here, and we're gonna have to call an ambulance—you got that?"

Christophe nodded. He was still crying.

"All right—so Odette's somewhere over by the cathedral?"

Christophe nodded again, this time pointing to the empty train tracks. "Met—"

"The Cathedral Metro station?"

Another nod.

"This is it," Art said to Lily. "We're at it."

Although they were holding him up, Christophe was

sagging toward the ground.

"Bench," Lily said.

Somehow they got him there. He leaned his head against Lily's shoulder.

"So you think she's here someplace?" Lily said. "And there's evil people in here you don't want her hanging out with." She felt a pang of fear as she looked around. All the Metro stations they had been in with Christophe had looked no better than this, but she felt a sudden pang of fear.

"Oh, man," Art said.

His eyes met Lily's over Christophe's head. She mouthed a "what?"

Art lowered his voice even more. "That first day when Pastor Renee was yelling at Odette, I caught a couple words, but I thought he was just mad because she got the tattoo. I mean, I knew he was trying to keep her out of trouble." His eyes were afraid. "Man—Lil—this could be serious."

"Yes! Please—" Christophe said. He gasped again, and then again.

"Art!" Lily said.

"Okay—okay—we gotta stay calm. All right—" He closed his eyes for a moment and breathed, "Dear God—Dear God—okay." He looked at Lily. "Three things have to happen. We have to tell Pastor Renee so he can run Odette down before the cops pick her up or something. We have to get Christophe out of here so he can breathe—preferably to Mom. And then—"

He licked his lips and groped for the words, and Lily knew what the third thing was.

"You're having an insulin reaction, aren't you?"

Art nodded. Panic hit Lily like a train, but she nodded as if she knew exactly what to do. It was her turn to whisper, "Dear God," and she added, "I wish I had a piece of candy or something."

Christophe wheezed louder and patted his pocket. Lily dove for it and pulled out a flattened square of chocolate. Her own hands were shaking almost as hard as Art's were as she bypassed them and stuck the candy right into his mouth.

Art chewed, and Lily watched until the color came back into his face. On the bench below them, Christophe sounded like he was fighting for breath.

"I'll try to get him up the steps," Art said. His voice was shaky now, and a little thick. "You run ahead, find a phone, and call Mom at the mission. Tell her to get Pastor Renee down here and then you come back and help me. And bring me a Coke or something. Here—here's some change."

Art's hand was clammy as he pressed a handful of Euros into her palm.

"Are you still having a reaction?" she said.

"I'm fine—just go!"

Lily dodged around people as she tore up the stairs toward the street. All of them now looked like they could perform evil even she couldn't imagine, and the panic rose up in her again.

You can't panic! You can't. Think. Think—one detail at a time!

Details. She grabbed onto the familiar thought as if it were a rope dangling from a lifeboat.

That's God talking, she thought. *God talks in the details!*

She stopped at the top of the steps. First detail. Telephone.

Lily spotted one across the street and ran for it, the change still clutched in her hand. She willed her fingers to stop shaking as she dropped the coins into the slot and punched out the numbers.

Now all you have to do is tell Mom, she told herself. *Just tell her every single thing. She and Pastor Renee will come, and it will all be over.*

But the phone rang endlessly on the other end, and then there was a click. Pastor Renee's recorded voice came on, speaking in French.

No, Lily wanted to shout at it. *Somebody real pick up the phone!*

But the beep sounded, and the tape hummed, waiting for her message.

Details, Lily thought. It was the only thing keeping her from crying.

"Mom," she said. "We're at the Notre Dame Metro Station. Christophe thinks Odette could be here, and she could be in trouble, so we need Pastor Renee. And Christophe can hardly breathe because he has asthma, so we need you too. And Art is having an insulin reaction. He's had one square of chocolate, but I'm getting him a Coke now. So—get here soon, okay, Mom?" Then she took a deep breath and hung up.

"Okay," she said out loud. "Somebody'll come to the phone and check it soon. It'll be all right. Just get Art a Coke."

A few people looked at her curiously as she crossed the street, but thinking out loud was making her feel better. She was doing it. She was working out the details. Now—a Coke for Art. She looked around and saw a café kitty-corner from where she stood. With a quick glance to see which light was green, she started across the street to her left. That was when she caught the flash of red hair on the other corner at the bus stop.

A detail. Red hair. Red hair that was so rare in Paris.

The bus sighed to a stop as Lily crossed the street

toward it. The knot of waiting people began to board, and the owner of the red hair followed, one foot up on the step. Lily stared at a detail that took her breath away—a boot, with a heel as high and thin as a pencil.

A horn blared as Lily ignored the light and tore across the street for the bus. The doors were slowly sighing closed as Lily lunged for the step and hurled herself inside. Her change flew out of her hand and scattered over the floor. She picked up enough to drop into the slot and then turned to look for Odette. She sat five rows back, her eyes boring right into Lily.

There was one detail Lily hadn't thought of—what she was going to do now. But still she moved, one step at a time, down the aisle until she was sitting in the seat across from Odette.

She wasn't looking at Lily anymore, but she did cross one leg over the other so that one pointy heel stuck out in the aisle like a weapon. Lily tried not to look at it.

"Odette?" Lily said.

The girl didn't answer, and Lily thought for a minute that maybe she had the wrong person. But the tattoo was there, and so were the eyes, which were now sweeping the view outside the window.

"Christophe is looking for you."

Odette's head jerked, and she almost looked at Lily. But she set her chin quickly and focused her eyes on the back of the driver's head.

"He figured out you're still in Paris. He doesn't want you getting in trouble around here with the evil people."

"Go away, enfant."

Lily felt the bus lurch as the driver pulled away from the curb. "I can't exactly do that. We're on a moving bus."

"Go away—and do *not* tell Christophe you saw me here.

If you do, you know I can hurt you."

"He needs you, Odette."

"I will get money to him. Now go away. This is no business of yours. You have only filled his mind with things that only build up his hopes about a God who does not care about him or me."

She stood up then and moved toward the front of the bus. The driver glanced curiously in his mirror and swerved toward the curb he had only just left a block before.

Lily got up too, grabbing for a pole as the bus lurched to a stop.

"He's sick, Odette!" she said. "Christophe can't breathe."

Odette whirled around, her eyes already drilling into Lily. "You are a liar!" she said.

"I'm not! He took us to the Cathedral Metro station where he thought you were, and by the time we got there, he was wheezing!"

The driver barked something at Odette in French. She didn't answer him but instead bore down on Lily, grabbing onto the back of a seat as the driver pulled the bus back into the traffic, muttering under his breath.

"Why did he go there?" she said.

"Because he figured it out. He thought about your tattoo and then he knew you never meant to leave France at all. But he knew you were just trying to make him think you were!"

"Where is he now?"

"He's at the Cathedral Metro Station—I told you that! He *needs* you, Odette!"

"*Halte!*" Odette shouted at the driver.

He shouted back in French, but Odette staggered to the front of the bus and banged on the door. The driver jerked the bus to the curb once more, and Odette jumped off with Lily right behind her.

Odette bullied her way through the crowd on the side-walk, bouncing off of their shoulders and bruising them with her elbows. Lily dodged several purses and at least one insult intended for Odette as she followed her. There was something different in Odette's manner now. The heels didn't clack the ground in anger. There was fear in the sound and in the way Odette bent her now-red head toward the Metro station.

And there was more fear in the cry that escaped her lips when she saw what Lily saw beneath the sign—two gendarmes and Art, crouched over the very still form of Christophe on the ground.

Fifteen

There were no details during the next several hours—not that Lily could remember. There was no need for them, because everything was being taken care of by hands and voices Lily could not have identified later if she had strained her brain.

Somehow Mom and Pastor Renee were suddenly there at the Metro station with them, just as the men with the ambulance were sliding Christophe into the back on a stretcher, an oxygen mask over his blue-pale face. Mom climbed into the front seat and was gone again. Pastor Renee packed Odette into his car and followed. But first, he chattered out French to a gendarme, who tucked Lily and Art into a taxi with a container of orange juice for Art and enough money to get them back to the apartment.

And for once, Lily didn't *want* to remember the details. Especially not the way Christophe looked when they closed the ambulance doors behind him.

When they were finally home and had explained all they could to a white-faced Joe and Tessa, Art told the pair of them to go in the kitchen and make some sandwiches. Miraculously, they did it without question. Lily waited until Art had closed the pass-through before she whispered to him, "You don't think Christophe's going to die, do you?"

Art shook his head as he joined her on the couch. "They didn't go racing to the hospital with the sirens going. I don't think people die of asthma if it's taken care of."

"What about Odette? You think she's gonna go to jail for stealing my passport?"

"She didn't actually try to use it." Art ran his hand back through his red curls. "You know what the real bummer is?"

"No."

"There's nothing else we can do."

Lily nodded. "A year ago, I'd be calling up the Girlz, coming up with some kind of plan. A month ago, I'd be running over to Sister Benedict's, all freaking out."

"What did you two do over there, anyway?"

"We talked. And we'd light candles and pray."

Art folded his arms. "That doesn't sound like a bad idea, actually. Mom doesn't have any candles, does she?"

"I do!" Lily bolted up to a sitting position. "Sister Benedict gave me some to take to Paris, and I haven't even used them. I am *so* gonna go pray right now."

"That is just like a woman," Art said.

"What is?"

"I give you an idea and you go off and do it like it was yours. Ever think I might wanna pray?"

"With *me*?" Lily said. "You want to do the candles and everything?"

"Yeah." Art was suddenly serious. "Yeah, I do."

So Lily pulled her candles from her pilgrimage satchel and brought them out of her room. Art had an end table cleared off and had moved it in front of the sofa. He watched her as she knelt down and arranged the candles in reverent silence. Their smell took Lily straight to the

Sister's little cell, where she could hear her saying, *Come, Holy Spirit, come.*

"Yes," Art whispered.

"What's burning?" Lily heard Joe say in the kitchen.

She and Art bowed their heads and were quiet. There was a lot of bumping and whispering from the other side of the pass-through, and then Lily felt Tessa's warm sweatiness beside her.

"Are we doing the Sister Benedict thing?" she whispered to Lily.

"No," Lily said. "We're doing the God thing."

They prayed—and they prayed—and they prayed. Lily didn't open her eyes or lift her head. She wasn't sure about the rest of her family, although Tessa barely wiggled and Joe even joined in with, "Please help Chris, God, 'cause he rocks."

When Lily whispered the "amen"—which everyone seemed to be waiting for her to do—Tessa picked up the snuffer and looked at Lily.

"Sure, go ahead," Lily said.

"Let the light of Jesus be in our hearts today, O God, our Father," Tessa said with her, "and let it guide our way."

"Amen to that."

Mom was standing in the doorway, and Lily was sure she saw tears in her eyes.

"He didn't die, did he?" Tessa said.

"No," Mom said. "And he isn't going to. He's out of danger. He's going to be fine."

"Yes!" Joe said.

He and Tessa high-fived each other. Art squeezed the bridge of his nose with two fingers. Lily started to cry.

"I don't get girls," Joe said.

Lily wanted to go and see Christophe right away, but

Mom said it would be best to make sure he was completely calm and rested before he had any excitement. Lily suspected it was *her* that Mom wanted calm and rested. She had a hard time not crying every ten minutes and just as hard a time falling asleep that night.

Has anything really changed for Christophe, God? she wrote in her journal. *Odette probably still wants to go do whatever it was she was going to do at the Metro—and Christophe still doesn't have parents to take care of him—and he still doesn't trust you. What did we really do?*

She closed the journal on her pen and looked down into the alley below. There were no cats tonight and no possibility that a freckle-nosed boy with the cutest accent in the world would appear from amid the trash cans and shinny up the pole to reach her. Oh, how she was going to miss France!

Lily leaned back against the window frame and drank in the details—the soft velvet of the Paris night air, the hum of the street beyond the alley, where nobody talked above a murmur even as they bought their peaches and sipped their "mud" in the café, the smell of milled soap on Tessa's fresh-bathed skin as she lay sleeping just a few feet from Lily's knees, the muffled sound of Art's singing from the loft above.

Art singing—making music again.

Lily flipped open her journal and grabbed the pen.

Art's going to be okay, isn't he, God? Somehow, you got him back. He said I helped with that, only I didn't even know it. I was just on my journey, picking up my details like Sister Benedict said. I wish the same thing would happen with Christophe.

No, God, I don't wish it. I pray it.

The next morning, Mom took Art and Lily to the hospital.

"I'm just going to drop you two off," she said, "and the two little squirts and I are going on an errand. We'll be back for you shortly."

"Why are we the squirts?" Joe said.

"And how come we don't get to see Christophe?"

"The French medical world isn't ready for the two of you yet," Mom said. It was good to see her lips twitching again, Lily decided. It was a nice detail.

Christophe was lying in bed, looking out the window, when they got to his room.

"Look at this," Art said. "You being still. They got you on drugs or something?"

"I brought you this," Lily said. She set a bag on his table. "It's a whole *loaf* of pain chocolat. You have to share it with me, though."

He smiled at them, but it wasn't a Christophe, what-shall-we-do-next smile. It made Lily as sad as if he had broken down and cried.

"What's up, dude?" Art said. "You in pain?"

Christophe shook his head. He looked at Art and then at Lily with that searching look, as if he were trying to see answers in their faces.

But he hasn't even asked a question! Lily thought.

"Come on, dude, dish," Art said. "It's us."

"Christophe," Lily said slowly. "They aren't taking you away when you get better, are they?"

"No. No—that is happy thing." He smiled a little. "I will stay with Pastor Renee and Madame Veronique until—"

He stopped, and a shadow passed over his face.

"Until what?" Art said.

"Until Odette, she can return."

"From where?"

"From the place where she must go." Christophe sighed as if the air were coming from his toes. "She came today—with Pastor Renee—to say good-bye. He has find the place she will go for the girls who—" Christophe shrugged.

"Girls who get really confused," Lily finished for him. "Because they don't have a mom to teach them not to wear killer heels and get tattoos and hang around in the Metro station."

"That is right?" Christophe said.

"That's what I'm thinkin'," Lily said.

Christophe sighed again and closed his eyes. Art leaned close to Lily.

"Good call, Lil," he whispered.

But when Christophe opened his eyes, they still searched Art and Lily as if he were longing for them to tell him something.

What does he want? Lily thought.

"So—did you get to say good-bye to her?" Art said.

Christophe nodded. "She make the—what is word—ah, the promise to not to continue this—confused."

"She'll get her act together," Art said. "She's a sharp kid. If she's as smart about doing the right thing as she was about doing the wrong thing, there won't be any stopping her."

But Christophe was shaking his head. "She is no like Li-lee. She is no—gather the details about God."

"She doesn't know how yet," Art said. "But they'll teach her at this place she's going to. Pastor Renee wouldn't send her there if it wasn't that kind of place."

"You are thinking this?" Christophe said.

"I'm definitely thinking this," Art said.

Christophe nodded, but his face was still drawn up into a question.

"So—you want to get in on some of this chocolate bread action?" Art reached for the bag, but Christophe suddenly squeezed his eyes shut.

"No!" he said.

"Okay, hands off the bread," Art said. He backed away from the table.

"No-no-no! Not bread—I want to know this. Li-lee—"

Lily looked helplessly at Art, but he shrugged and nodded her toward the bed. Lily crept up to Christophe's side. He opened his eyes and curled his fingers around her sleeve, pulling her closer.

"I am listen for God," he said. "And I think, yes, I know, like you, Li-lee."

"That's good, Christophe." She whispered, because it suddenly didn't seem right to talk out loud.

"You say I do not have to be good Christophe to hear God?"

"Right. You just have to believe in Christ, and then you *will* be 'good Christophe.' When I can't figure something out, I read my Bible and listen for what God is telling me. He teaches me how to see him—all the time."

"And Odette? She does not believe. Will she never be 'good Odette'?"

Lily felt as tangled up as Christophe's own words. How could she answer that? And then she knew. The only way she could.

"Well," she said. "You have to pray for her, of course. And then you know how we looked for God with you, you know, in all the little stuff I was gathering?"

Christophe nodded.

"You just have to do that with her."

"But she is no here."

"So you store it all up 'til she comes back. You tell

her how much God loves her, just the way we told you."

He pulled himself halfway up and looked around the room. There were three other beds there, two of them empty. The other had a curtain around it and voices muttering behind it.

"Nothing here," Christophe said. He sank back into his pillows, but his eyes had taken on a tiny Christophe-twinkle.

"You see something," Lily said. She could feel herself starting to grin.

"I see God," he said. He looked at her, and his eyes weren't searching anymore. "I see God in the eyes of Li-lee. Trés magnifique."

Lily could feel herself blushing from the tips of her toes.

"Anybody want some bread?" Art said.

There was a tap on the door soon after that. It was Joe and Tessa, ready for their turn with Christophe. They were loaded down with bags of stuff for him, and they looked like they were about to burst with some pent-up secret.

"You have to go down to the lobby and see Mom," Tessa said, shoving Lily toward the door.

"What's the big deal?" Lily said.

But when the elevator doors opened for her and Art on the lobby floor, she knew. There was Dad, and peeking out from behind him was someone else—someone who ran to her with her arms thrown out to her.

"*Reni?*" Lily cried. "*Reni?*"

"Sure looks like her to me," Art said.

But Lily hardly heard him. She was crying much too hard.

It was four days before Lily even caught her breath. But it was all right not to breathe when everything was Paris-magical and best-friend-beautiful, from the croissants and hot chocolate in the café every morning to the late-night talks in the bedroom window with their feet dangling down over the alley. Lily told Reni everything. Absolutely everything. Lily hadn't realized how many details there were until she had to tell them all to Reni.

Reni had details too, of course, and they shared those as they climbed every step to the top of the Eiffel Tower and lay on their backs in the grass in the Tuileries and stood looking at the Mona Lisa in the Louvre. Mom said she never saw two people who could talk so much. But Lily had to hear it all.

She had to hear how Zooey had gone out for junior varsity cheerleader for next year—and made it. "Who would have thought?" Lily said.

"Everybody," Reni said. "She was wonderful at the tryouts. Our Zooey."

And then she heard about how Suzy had made the soccer team—no big surprise—and how she had been elected co-captain. A freshman. Their shy Suzy. *Big* surprise.

And then she sat captivated as Reni told her how Kresha was now speaking rings of English around people like Chelsea and Ashley, who now said "like" every other word and had gotten demoted to regular English for high school because they didn't do their homework half the time. Before they knew it, Reni predicted, Kresha herself would be in honors—with them.

And then, of course, Lily wanted to hear about Shad Shifferdecker.

"He's still a goofball," Reni said. "But a pretty decent goofball." And Reni told Lily that he asked at least once a week when she would be coming home.

"You *are* coming home soon," Reni said to Lily the night Dad took them all to see *The Barber of Seville* at the Opera.

Lily was so thrilled just to be seeing the opera house again, much less be sitting in a red velvet seat waiting for the curtain to open, that she had to blink several times at Reni to realize what she had said.

"I am, aren't I?" she said. "Wow."

Reni nodded. She was watching Lily closely.

"You're happy about that, aren't you? I mean, I know I haven't written to you that much. It was hard, especially when I knew I was coming, and I had to keep it a secret. I knew I'd blab it all over the place if I wrote too many emails."

"It's okay," Lily said. "It was worth it."

The lights began to dim, and an excited hush fell over the audience. Reni reached over and squeezed her hand.

"I have missed you *so* much, Lil," she whispered. "I can't wait 'til you get home and everything is the same again."

On the other side of her, Lily heard a grunt. She looked over in time to see Art giving her a glance before the overture began, and the world was transformed.

Lily had never seen—or heard—anything more glorious than what was on the stage that night. She didn't understand most of it, since it was sung in Italian and the words flashed up on the screen were in French, but that didn't seem to matter. She laughed and nudged Reni and leaned her head over to Art to have him explain something now and then.

During the first intermission, Mom led all the girls to the restroom.

"I'm about to pop," Reni said.

Lily was going to follow her in when she saw Art go by, hands in the pockets of his dress slacks, head bent in a way Lily hadn't seen it in a while.

"I'll be right back," Lily said to Reni.

And then she wove her way through the crowd, careful not to jostle silk-covered elbows as she went to where she knew Art would be. She sat down on the step beside him.

It was not as quiet as it had been that day she'd found him in this same spot—the day he'd told her, "I need music." But the Paris murmur faded around them as they sat together now, side by side.

It was Art who spoke first. "I got to thinking about what Reni said to you about everything being the same when you get home." He shook his head.

"It won't be, will it?" Lily said.

"I hope not. I'm just afraid I'm not going to be able to hold onto the beauty, you know?"

Lily did know, and she nodded.

"I found somebody creative inside myself here," he went on. "I'm writing songs now. Songs for God. That's something I always wanted to do."

"That rocks," Lily said.

"That's the idea." He gave a half grunt. "But can I do it? It's easy here—this is Paris, for Pete's sake. Stuff changes all the time. Things won't be the same—I won't be the same when we get home." Art turned his head to grin at her. "I can't believe I'm asking my kid sister this."

"I can," Lily said, "because I think I know the answer."

"So dish."

Lily smoothed her palms over the flare of the skirt that spilled out from her lap to the plush carpet they sat on. "Sister Benedict says that things change all the time. But the one thing that doesn't is God and your true self that he made you to be. I think you probably found your true self while we were gathering up God's details, and that's gonna go everywhere with you."

They were quiet for a while, until the lights dimmed and then grew bright again.

"That means it's time for the next act," Lily said. "Dad told me that."

She started to stand up, but Art caught her sleeve.

"I think you've found your true self too, Lil. You know, that *you* you've been looking for ever since you thought you were gonna be some fashion model?"

Lily nodded.

"The real Lily Robbins is this trés magnifique person who is probably gonna do about a hundred different things with her life before she's through. But her true thing? It's always gonna be gathering up the details and sorting them out and doing what God tells her in that whole big basket of stuff only she and God understand." He shook his curly head. "Does that make any sense at all?"

"Yeah," Lily said, in a voice full of happiness-tears.

And it did. Of course, it did.

Because it was a God thing.

Dear Fellow Friends of Lily,

If you're like me, you're a little bummed out that this is the last book in the Lily Series. After all, we've been with her through the major events that have shaped her as a person. This must be what Lily felt like when she had to say good-bye to Christophe and Kimble and Ingram and Sister Benedict. We're saying good-bye to a friend we're never going to see again (unless we read her stories over and over again, which isn't a bad idea!!).

Maybe it'll make us all feel better to know what became of Lily after she left Paris and Oxford and returned to the United States. I happen to have the inside scoop!

When Lily got back to Oxford, Ingram and Kimble were getting along a lot better. They both went with the Robbins family when they visited Scotland, Ireland, Wales, and even Holland. Lily, of course, gathered God details the entire time and had plenty to take back to Burlington, New Jersey, to share with her Girlz. The group of old friends stayed together through high school, although their interests led them in different directions sometimes.

Reni was totally into orchestra and was accepted at Juilliard—only one of THE most famous music schools in the whole country—right after graduation. Lily's brother Art was pretty jealous, although he didn't do too badly himself, going to the University of Southern California and then becoming a world-class composer of contemporary Christian music.

Suzy really excelled at sports, especially soccer. Because she was captain of the girls' team, she got over her shyness and went on to Trenton State College to train as a high school coach.

Kresha made it into high school honors classes and

could speak not only English, but enough French, Spanish, and German by the time she graduated to know she wanted to become an international interpreter. She joined the Navy and was sent almost immediately to the language school in Monterey, California. Guess where all the Girlz went on their first college spring break?!

Zooey was probably the biggest surprise. She got into the beauty pageant scene and was crowned Miss Burlington, which not only meant she went on to the Miss New Jersey pageant, but she won a full college scholarship. She didn't become Miss New Jersey, but she did go to fashion design school and has a promising career. She's assured all the Girlz that she'll design and make their wedding dresses when the time comes for them to get married.

Speaking of marriage, Lily and Shad Shifferdecker did become an item their junior and senior years in high school, but when they both went their separate ways after graduation, they decided not to make a commitment to one another. They agreed that if God wanted them to be together forever, he would see that it happened. Oh yeah. Shad did become a Christian while Lily was in England. Who would have thought, huh? (Well, obviously, God did!)

And Lily? Her high school years were a wonderful mixture of God things. She continued to be involved in theater. She wrote for the high school paper and was a class officer every year, and, of course, made amazing grades. But her biggest thing was her pilgrimage with God. Lily took a mission trip every summer, headed up her youth group, and mentored a lot of younger kids who were just discovering the presence of God.

Lily was definitely a huge influence on Tessa, who started a Christian athletes group in middle school when she got there and fought—as only Tessa could do—for the right of her fellow athletes to pray together in the locker room before games. Even Joe got into it—although to this day, he still claims that his sister Lily is "weird." If weird means that you grow up to attend a Christian college and become a writer and speaker whose ministry is called "Growing Up Is a God-Thing," then, yeah, I guess she's pretty weird.

I do miss Lily now that she's all grown up. In fact, I was talking to her the other day (NOW who's weird?!), and she asked me to tell you two things:

1. Continue to learn about God and how he works in the lives of girls just like you by reading the Faithgirlz Sophie Series. (Lily *highly* recommends it!) Sophie LeCroix, who lives in Virginia, is a creative dreamer, almost certainly destined to become a great film director someday. The first two books are *Sophie's World* and *Sophie's Secret*.

2. Keep praying, keep journaling, keep reading your Bible, and keep gathering those details about God, and he will whisper his love and his wisdom to you.

> Blessings on you,
> my fellow Lily-friends,
> Nancy Rue

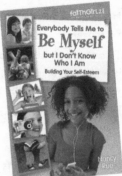

faiThGirLz!
the beauty of believing

Devotions

No Boys Allowed Devotions for Girls

Softcover

This short, ninety-day devotional for girls ages 10 and up is written in an upbeat, lively, funny, and tween-friendly way, incorporating the graphic, fast-moving feel of a teen magazine.

Rock Devotions for You

Softcover

In this ninety-day devotional, devotions like "Who Am I?" help pave the spiritual walk of life, and the "Girl Talk" feature poses questions that really bring each message home. No matter how bad things get, you can always count on God.

Chick Chat More Devotions for Girls

Softcover

This ninety-day devotional brings the Bible right into your world and offers lots to learn and think about.

Shine On, Girl! Devotions to Keep You Sparkling

Softcover

This ninety-day devotional will "totally" help teen girls connect with God, as well as learn his will for their lives.

Available now at your local bookstore!
Visit www.faithgirlz.com. It's the place for girls ages 9-12.

Talk It Up!

Want free books?
First looks at the best new fiction?
Awesome exclusive merchandise?

We want to hear from you!

Give us your opinions on titles, covers, and stories.
Join the Z Street Team.

Email us at zstreetteam@zondervan.com
to sign up today!

Also—Friend us on Facebook!

www.facebook.com/goodteenreads

- Video Trailers
- Connect with your favorite authors
- Sneak peeks at new releases
- Giveaways
- Fun discussions
- And much more!